where memories live

Kathy G. Widener

Kathy G Widener

Deeds Publishing | Atlanta

Published by Deeds Publishing in Athens, GA
www.deedspublishing.com

Printed in The United States of America

Cover design by Mark Babcock
Text layout by Ashley Clarke

Library of Congress Cataloging-in-Publications data is available upon request.

ISBN 978-1-947309-15-9

Books are available in quantity for promotional or premium use. For information, email info@deedspublishing.com.

First Edition, 2017

10 9 8 7 6 5 4 3 2 1

In memory of
my uncle,
Leon Odell Gantt
&
my daddy,
ꓙbert Kelly Gantt

Preface

MY UNCLE LEON GANTT HAD A PHENOMENAL MEMORY AND could remember when and where an event took place, and the people involved. Most of the time, he could remember the day, month, year, and even the weather. He was an avid storyteller and relished the telling. I always enjoyed the stories he told, particularly about making moonshine and running from Revenuers. The stories were certainly entertaining, as were the characters. My sisters and I used to write down his stories or tape them so we would not miss any important details. After he passed away in 2002 at the age of 91, I decided his stories were entertaining enough to be shared, so I began writing this book

When I finally finished the book, it was entirely too long, so I decided the best action would be to make it two books, which I have done. Now it has developed into the Rayflin Series, a trilogy. This book, *Rayflin: Where Memories Live* is book one chronicling the Gantt family and their life of back-breaking work on a five-hundred-acre farm, living with the changes of seasons so important to farm life. It was a sunup to sundown job and a poignant story of the realities of country life in the early twentieth century. It describes their joy at birth and how quickly that joy can turn to sorrow in death. They lived through the flu pandemic of 1918, when thousands died, and World War I, when thousands more were sacrificed on the altar of freedom in foreign lands. All events depicted are true, but when covering a span of years so far in the past, some allowances had to be made. All the main characters really lived in the Rayflin and the Sugar Bottom area of Lexington County, S.C. near the banks of the North Edisto River. The small communities mentioned in my book, Rayflin, Sugar Bottom, Seivern, and the Chalk Hill Mine, are gone now, and there are only a meager few living persons who recall their importance. I thought their stories needed to be told.

Depending mostly on my Uncle's storytelling gift, which was awesome, I wove his stories into a narrative that gives insight into the lives of my family. A family saga, so to speak, with pictures included of all the main characters. When you can read about a character and really see how that character looked, it makes the story becomes more visual and interesting. These were a hardworking, stubborn, and in most cases, hard drinking people.

Book II, Rayflin: The Return Home is completed and hopefully will go to press within a reasonable amount of time. *The Return Home* continues their story, including how they were affected by the stock market crash, the Great Depression—when there were no jobs to be had to support their families—and during Prohibition, when moonshine was in great demand. The production of moonshine became their livelihood. 'Desperate times call for desperate measures,' and these were desperate times. There was always someone willing to pay for liquor, and Leon became the best in the business. He said to me, "Jack Daniels can't make liquor stronger than I can. I can taste the water in a stream and tell if it's good to make moonshine with."

The main characters were real people, who were mostly my family. The events recorded in these books happened in that time and place. I did create the character of Sibbie, who stayed with Mary while her husband was away. Sibbie came to help Mary with the children and the chores. The other members of Sibbie's family were real people who lived and worked on the farm at Rayflin. The book mentions Jennie Lou, Uncle Caesar, Aunt Maggie, Aunt Chaney, and Willie Burkett, the black man who plays a prominent role in one of my favorite stories. Aunt Chaney was a Gantt, her daughter Maggie's children, Jennie Lou and Willie's father was a Burkett. I invented Sibbie as another daughter of Maggie's because her real daughter, Jennie Lou, was much younger at the time, too young to work and live with Mary. I wanted to fashion the personality of a fictional character rather than speculate on or change a true person. The other black families working at Rayflin are also fictitious, at least in their names. The exception was Arthur Moore, who did work for Mr. Kel on the farm and lived in the small house mentioned in the book. Other minor characters' names, even though they existed in Uncle Leon's accounts, have been lost in antiquity, so the names are fictitious. An example is the two men who worked for the Pond Branch Telephone Company. The story happened just the way it is recorded, but the names I invented. And the date of the actual telephone connection is uncertain; my father said there was a phone in the old house in 1912.

World War II and its effect on the Gantts is a big part of *The Return Home*. Leon served his country in North Africa and Italy in the 5th Army under General Mark Clark, of whom he spoke highly. He told stories about the War, events he experienced and where he was at the time. They definitely were not all good memories; he included those memories most soldiers would want to forget. I had to do research and take certain liberties with the "when and where" of events he had told us about. I tried to follow Sergeant Leon Gantt through the War in North Africa and Italy and stay away from technical matters and actions unrelated to him.

In the stories detailed in the Rayflin series, I do not use proper grammar—the story is written in the local vernacular of the people depicted. All the stories told are true per my uncle and father.

I'm tremendously grateful to Uncle Leon for all the stories he passed on, and also my father Robert, who was a good storyteller as well. He was not as forthcoming with his stories as his brother. He had to be asked about particulars, and then he would gladly share, whereas Uncle Leon loved to talk about his moonshining exploits and his war experience.

The trilogy I promised concludes with *Rayflin: Southern Child, A Memoir*. It's my story about spending the first twelve years, my childhood, in that same old house my grandfather, Kelly, and his brothers built in 1912. We did have electricity beginning in 1948, but being born in 1951, I remember no indoor plumbing, and no heating or cooling except burning wood in the winter and opening the windows in the sultry heat of July and August. Everybody has a story, so I intend to tell mine. I have begun and intend to finish. So many people have lived in the lap of luxury growing up; my brother, sisters, and I lived in that same old unpainted house, much like my grandparents.

I hope the reader will enjoy what I have written, knowing that most of it is absolutely true. Remembering stories from the past leads to an appreciation of what our families endured and their memories live on through the telling of them to others.

K.G. Widener
July 24, 2017

One

STREAMS OF RAIN CASCADED DOWNWARD FROM THE EAVES
of the kitchen house. The woman stood in front of the wood cook
stove inside; she was intent on the job at hand, preparing supper
for her husband. It was unseasonably cold for a mid-October afternoon, and the sound of the rain beating on the roof above added
to the chill that seeped into every crack and cranny of the old
building.

The kitchen house where she now stood was a separate building,
set longways behind the two rooms of the main house. The chimney
was up against the main house Kelly, her husband, and his brothers
Roston, Sam, and Woodard had completed only three years before.
The chimney was sand rock, mud, and limestone. There was a string
latch on the front door, the shuttered windows were closed with
homemade hinges of oak, and the roof was covered with shaker
cedar shingles.

The woman's name was Mary, and her protruding belly gave
testimony that the time was near for her to birth her first child.

"How wonderful the heat rising from the wood stove feels bath-
ing my face and upper body," Mary whispered under her breath.

Standing there cooking and listening to the drumming on the

roof above, she could feel the tendrils of her dark hair hanging limply on either side of her face.

Mary thought to herself in exasperation, *The bun I twisted and pulled my hair into on top of my head this morning is beginning to come loose as the steam rising from the cook stove fills the air with moisture. If only I had someplace to adjust the hairpins out here in the kitchen house; it would look so much better when Kelly gets home. I know my hair looks like a disheveled wreck, and I would so like for Kelly to notice my appearance when he returns from down at the farm.* She had been alone all day and only had herself to talk to.

Before Kelly left for the farm early that morning, he had cut two collards from the garden some two hundred feet from the kitchen house, down a slope near the spring. Walking back up the slope from the spring, a sudden rain shower hit and he had to run, hopping onto the porch out of the cold shower.

A rain barrel sat on the ground at the corner of the kitchen house porch and was kept full from the streams that ran off down the roof. Every time rain fell, water would spill right into the barrel.

"Thought we might have these collards for supper," Kelly had remarked. "They should be good, since that frost last week fell on them. Pa always says, 'Greens aren't nearly as good until a good frost falls on the leaves.' Do you feel like fooling with them? If not, I'll take them to Rayflin for Ma. I know the baby is due soon. Maybe you should just take it easy."

"I'm fine, Kelly, and if you'll help get them ready, I can do the rest," was Mary's reply. "I'm quite capable even in my condition, you know. But I would appreciate your help getting them ready before you go, and your concern too, for my condition, of course. You could help by removing some of the hard stems."

"Of course, I'd be happy to," he replied.

Kelly cut the hard stalks from the collards and trimmed the thick ribs of the leaves. All this excess went into the slop bucket beside the small table on the porch, to be dumped in the trough for their hogs later. Kelly even went inside and brought out two dishpans and a dipper to fill the pans with rain water from the barrel. Everything was ready for the preparation. "Don't try to pour the water out when you are through," warned Kelly. "They'll be too heavy for you to be lifting; I'll see to that when I get back from Rayflin this afternoon. Promise me? I'll empty the slop bucket before I go," he added.

"OK. I'll leave them right here for you to empty," Mary replied. "But I'm not helpless, only pregnant."

During the bleak morning hours, Mary spent her time with daily cleaning chores. First, she worked in the kitchen house, cleaning up from their breakfast of grits and fried fatback, and then she splashed through puddles from the kitchen house to the back steps of the main house, climbing the six slippery back steps. Her clothes were damp by the time she was inside; she had to be cautious climbing up the sodden wood steps. In her condition, one slip could be disastrous. Inside, she dried herself with a towel beside the wood stove, adding more wood, made their bed, and tidied up their room.

The rain poured on the tin roof and from the window, she could barely see the kitchen house through the curtain of water from above. The downpour lasted only for a short spell; she sat down in the rocker beside the stove, waited for a break in the sound of rain above, and let her clothing dry completely. When she heard a definite let-up in the rain hitting the roof, she decided to return to the

3

kitchen house. Now was the time to move; who knew when there would be another break in the storm?

The rest of the day she could remain in the kitchen house, spending the better part of the afternoon washing and chopping the collard leaves into small pieces to cook for their supper.

It was late on a Saturday afternoon, almost five o'clock. Gray and gloomy most of the day, the rain that had started early morning would continue throughout the afternoon.

The collards were now simmering on the back eye of the stove as she fried potatoes and hoecakes in two black iron skillets on the front. Kelly would be home anytime now, and Mary wanted to have his supper cooked when he returned.

The little building that she stood in was old and had been occupied by Demps Kneece, a veteran of the War Between the States. No one knew exactly how old it really was, but the building's main support beams were put together with oak pegs and lx4 inch heart pine lumber constructed with handmade square-head nails. A small porch with a little shed room at the end was the perfect place to store jars of canned vegetables, jams, and jellies, which sat on shelves on the back wall. There was also a salt box for preserving meat.

Mary looked around the room as she stood beside the stove. With the storm still raging outside, she thought, *How has this little one-room house withstood the weather and the ravages of time for so many years? And what drama and all manner of human misery and happiness have taken place here? If only these walls could talk, what a story they would tell.*

She continued her deep emotional assessment of her surroundings, needing the presence of another human to justify what seemed to her a wasted gloomy day. She continued pondering deep thoughts of the past. *This little building must be more than a hundred years old. It was a refuge surely for some interesting people. Confederate and most probably Yankee soldiers both were in this room, even quite possibly Indians in its early years. More recently, the little house has witnessed drunken visitors and a resident whore to entertain them. What a fascinating history.*

It was only 20x12 feet in size, probably considered a large cabin by the original occupants, but it now served as Kelly and Mary's kitchen. With a fireplace on the left wall that butted up against the main house, it also contained a wood cook stove, cook table, pie safe, table and chairs. It was an ideal kitchen, but its separation from their main house was an inconvenience.

Kelly and his brother, Roston, lived here for a while after their pa, Kel, ran Demps Kneece off the place. It seems Demps, his sister Lizzie, and her daughter Dorothy lived here together. Dorothy attracted lots of male attention in the community. She did a lot of entertaining and her uncle was too old to deal with the situation. Her mother just turned a blind eye to the goings-on.

Mr. Demps was quite the character himself and insisted he'd been at Appomattox when General Lee surrendered. "General Lee sat on that big grey horse under a Crabapple tree and cried like a baby," Demps would say. "The General sure loved his men. Only surrendered because we couldn't hold on any longer. We all respected and loved that man."

Demps tolerated Dorothy's behavior because he felt helpless to stop it; besides, all the male visitors kept him supplied with liquor, which he had grown accustomed to drinking on a daily basis. He had no qualms about the whoring. He had done his share as a young man, but he didn't approve of his niece's behavior. It was somehow different when it's your own flesh and blood. Truth be known, Kelly and his brothers had visited Dorothy themselves on occasion. Their Pa was unaware of their involvement with her.

After Demps, Lizzie and Dorothy departed; Kelly and Roston had approached Pa Kel about living in the small building.

"Pa, how about you allowing Roston and myself to stay in the little building batching it?" Kelly asked. "When we find the right woman, we'll make other arrangements. Meanwhile, we'll start building a main house with the help of Woodard and Sam." Kelly didn't hesitate to volunteer Sam and Woodard, because he knew they would be glad to help him and Roston build the two-room main house, if only to get out from under Kel's watchful eyes for a spell and all the chores he could find for them at Rayflin. Arrangements were finally agreed upon and Roston and Kelly took up residence a mile from their pa and ma. The main house was built and the little house became a separate kitchen.

Ulysses Kelly Gantt, called Kelly by family and friends, was an attractive man. He was medium height, which would have made him almost invisible to Mary when they first met. Then he doffed his gray derby hat, revealing straight blonde hair parted down the middle. It was the style of the time, but when she first looked into those gray-blue eyes and met that smile, she was completely and irreversibly drawn in. The eyes were what made her feel giddy. They were almost too pale, the color of a gray dawn with a definite blue lining the iris. She had never seen eyes the color of Kelly's, and those extraordinary eyes twinkled when he briefly bowed and said, "Ma'am, it is a pleasure to make the acquaintance of such a lovely lady." To Mary, the combination of his looks and manner of speech determined then and there he was the only man she could ever love.

She awaited his arrival that night in the kitchen house with anticipation, yearning for his companionship and some conversation after the gloom of a day filled only with chores to mark the passing hours. She'd not seen him since he'd left early that morning, soon after helping her with the greens. Kelly and his brothers helped their pa, Kel, down at the family's main farm a mile away. Kelly did farm some acreage in fields near his house with the help of their farmhands, but the bulk of farming was at his family's main residence at Rayflin, a mile away. Kelly also had a large barn, a couple of mules, a milk cow, some pigs, and a small flock of chickens that freely roamed the yard. Their chickens provided eggs and meat, and the cow provided milk. His farm operation was nothing, size wise, to the family's farmed acreage down the road. The entire family supported and worked the Rayflin acreage. *Thank goodness the cotton was picked before this rain,* Mary thought to herself. It was now in the wagons under the sheds at Mr. Kel's, waiting to be taken to the gin.

Mary, a stately woman of twenty-six, expected her first child any day now. She had dark hair, parted in the middle and pulled back in a bun on top of her head. Her finely chiseled features and creamy complexion made her something of a beauty, but life was hard for her now and her beauty would fade fast. Cooking, cleaning, feeding and caring for their animals, and everything else that goes with being a farmer's wife was already taking its toll. There were very few luxuries to be had in the backwoods of South Carolina, especially near the North Edisto river swamp in the year of 1910.

* * * * *

Her family had not approved of Kelly Gantt. He and his brothers had a reputation for drinking, gambling and consorting with the wrong kind of women. Mary had met him through a family connection, as was the beginning of many relationships in the South. Mary's first cousin, Jule Smith, son of her Uncle William, married Kelly's sister, Corrie. Although Mary's parents were fond of cousin Jule and his wife, that affection did not extend to Corrie's philandering, excessive-drinking brother, Kelly. After their first introduction at Jule and Corrie's house, Mary and Kelly would seemingly bump into each other whenever her family made their weekly trip to the dry goods store in Batesburg. Kelly was always there, smiling and making small talk with her parents while seemingly ignoring her presence. She did, however, notice the fleeting admiring glances he tossed in her direction. Kelly Gantt was no fool; he knew in order to get close to the daughter, he had to first impress her folks. He was polite and respectful towards them, frequently complimenting her mother.

"Mrs. Fink, you certainly look fetching today. Let me help carry your packages to the buggy," he would say.

Mary saw him there every Saturday and had come to look forward to his presence. After six months, he had asked her father, Frank Fink, for the privilege of calling on her, and her father reluctantly agreed.

She now stood in the kitchen of their home, cooking his supper and anticipating the birth of his child. The potatoes were ready, the collards were done, and the hoecakes were getting cold. "Where is he?" she asked herself. "It's pouring rain outside and the darkness is settling in—he should be home by now."

A sudden increase in the noisy clatter of rain hitting the roof, the draft of chill damp air bellowing Mary's skirts, and the creaking of door hinges interrupted her deep thoughts. Her senses followed the commotion as Kelly appeared in the doorway.

"Mary, how was your day? You didn't empty those dishpans, did you?" Kelly asked with his usual grin. "Pa had so much for us to do. You would think the work was mostly over since we are having this God-awful rain and cold, but you know how Pa is. Kelly continued, "He had us mending harnesses for all his mules, sharpening his plows in anticipation of next spring's planting, and we spent a goodly portion of the day shelling corn for the mules' feed and for seed corn. He says in a couple more weeks, we'll butcher those two hogs and that should give us plenty of meat for the winter."

My, but Kelly was talkative tonight. He hadn't even given her pause to answer his questions about how her day had been before he continued talking. Mary suspected he had plans with his brothers, especially since they had spent the day in one another's company. They had plenty of time to plan the mischief they would get into. It was, after all, Saturday night. All these thoughts were running through Mary's mind while Kelly was describing what happened at Rayflin. Kelly and his brothers had a moonshine still somewhere down in the swamp, she was sure of it, even though she had no idea where, and evidently neither did Mr. Kel. He did not allow that sort of thing at his place, the making of moonshine. If he found the still, he would bust it up with an axe. All the brothers knew their pa and knew what he would do. They kept its location a secret for a reason.

"Some of the boys are coming by after supper, if that's okay with you." Not waiting for Mary's approval, Kelly continued, "We thought we might play a hand of cards out here in the kitchen house. After supper, of course. The weather is so nasty outside; I told them I didn't think you would mind. Whenever you're ready to turn in, I'll escort you to the house and make sure you have a good fire before coming back to be with the boys." He knew Mary did not approve of card playing.

Mary immediately thought of the consequences of such behavior. Rumors of the card playing would spread, and the offender would be asked to atone in front of the church congregation for such behavior. Kelly wouldn't be present when that happened anyway. Mary was pretty certain. He seldom attended services with her any more. He went regularly before their marriage, but only to impress her folks and prove he was worthy of their daughter. After all, Mary's grandfather was the pastor, and Kelly had been intent on presenting a pious front.

All these thoughts were running through Mary's mind, but she thought it best to keep quiet. After Kelly had seen her to bed, then they could bring out the jug.

"Please not tonight, Kelly. It's been such a long day, and I so hoped you might attend services with me tomorrow."

She had barely gotten the protest from her lips when the first contraction hit. She continued putting the food on the table, silently hoping it was a false pain. The baby was not due for another two weeks; surely this couldn't be labor. She had even heard her mother speak of such pains as a normal thing when a woman's time was near. Then the spasm in her abdomen hit again and water started running down Mary's legs, puddling on the floor. Mary didn't just suspect this was labor: now she knew. Her water had broken and the pains continued to come closer together. This was the real thing. She tried to ignore the pains, but neither she nor Kelly could ignore the puddle on the floor. He saw the grimace of pain on her face, evidence that could not be ignored.

"Mary, are you in labor?"

"I'm sure I am, Kelly. You probably need to go fetch Miss Hannah right away. She will know what to do."

She wasn't ready, but then, would she ever be? It was an excruciating pain, and with the gush of water, there was no doubt now; it was her time. She was suddenly frightened by the inevitable.

Almost immediately, there was a knock on the door. Mary stood beside the table holding her belly, keenly aware of her wet skirts and the puddle of water at her feet.

Kelly threw open the door. It was Roston and Sam, ready for a game of cards and a night of drinking. *Uh, not tonight!*

"Mary is in labor, boys, I think our hand has already been dealt for tonight: a game of wait-and-see, not poker." Mary was mortified that Kelly's brothers should see her this way, but it couldn't be helped.

"Hold the door, Roston, I need to get Mary into the house. Sam, you go and fetch Miss Hannah."

Two

KELLY SCOOPED MARY UP INTO HIS ARMS AND HEADED OUT. He paused on the porch long enough to glance at Roston. "Light the lantern hanging outside the door. I don't want to stumble in a puddle with Mary in my arms crossing the yard. And hold that lantern high; those steps into the main house are bound to be slippery," Kelly reminded Roston.

Roston set the lantern on the table outside the door and lifted the glass chimney. A breeze was blowing, damp and heavy with moisture, but the chimney had kept the wick dry and he had no problem striking a match on the wall and lighting it. The rain was coming down pretty heavy still, pouring off the roof into the rain barrel. "If you don't mind, Roston, take off your coat and cover Mary," said Kelly anxiously. "It will help keep her dry until we can get her inside."

After Mary was covered with the coat, Roston hurriedly led the way down the two steps, holding the lantern high, before the little group huddled against the rain and wind. Mary had her arms around Kelly's neck, clinging to him like he was a life raft in the storm. She could only moan softly under the covering of Roston's coat, wishing their trip across the yard would be over quickly; her pains were increasing in intensity, along with her level of anxiety. She saw nothing but blackness but could hear the rain and wind surrounding them and feel the pelting drops on the rough cloth of Roston's coat.

Kelly knew they needed to hurry and get her out of the rain, but care had to be taken for Mary's condition. The little group moved fast through the drenching rain, across the yard, and up the six slick steps into the main house. Roston stood at the top and held the door open for Kelly, who was carrying Mary like a baby. Sam had already cranked their pa's Model T and was on the way to get Miss Hannah Wells, the local midwife.

When they entered the back door into their bedroom, Kelly put Mary gently on her feet. The room was in deep shadow. It was half past five in the evening, and with the rainy weather outside, the light was almost gone. After Roston held the outer door open for Kelly, he immediately disappeared into the other room, closing the door so they could be alone. A small fire still burned in the potbellied stove. Mary had added wood earlier in order to maintain at least a bed of embers for nighttime. Kelly helped her undress in the chill room and wrapped her in a quilt while he built up the fire.

"I'll just go ahead, Kelly, and make a fire in here," Roston called through the door.

The house consisted of only two rooms, both rooms used as sleeping quarters. A porch across the front faced the road and had two entrances. Kelly and Roston had built the house that way so they both had an entrance to their bedrooms. They had constructed the house in '07 and lived there together barely two years before Mary came. As soon as Kelly took a wife, Roston had moved back in with Pa and Ma at Rayflin.

There was a double fireplace between the rooms with one flue. On Roston's side, there was an open fireplace and in their room, a piece of tin fit the fireplace. The edge of the tin was bent a half-inch all the way round, so it fit snug into the opening. A hole for the stove pipe extending from the top of their small potbellied stove was vended through the insert and up the chimney.

Kelly helped Mary dry herself and put on her flannel nightdress. Picking up the heap of wet things from the floor, he draped them over a rocker beside the stove.

"Everything will be fine, Mary. Sam will be back soon with Miss Hannah," Kelly said as he turned back the quilts and helped Mary under the covers. He must've been trying to appear calm, hoping his words would help soothe her pains if he could keep his excitement manageable. "It looks like I'll be getting that son tonight."

Mary did not even hear his words. She was too absorbed in the pain that now racked her body.

Kelly sat beside the bed and took Mary's hand, trying to reassure her. "I've helped Pa deliver lots of heifers, Mary; it's just a natural process."

"Excuse me, Kelly Gantt, but I am not a heifer! You can't imagine the pain I'm having. God left childbearing to women for a good reason. He knew men couldn't endure this agony."

So much for trying to sound reassuring. Best thing to do is just shut up, he thought.

* * * * *

After what seemed an eternity to Mary, Sam got back with Miss Hannah. She came bustling into the room with the air of someone who is in charge and knows it.

"Kelly Gantt, get yourself out of here this instant. This is women's business. Just wait in the next room with those two trifling brothers of yours."

Kelly departed reluctantly, kissing Mary on the cheek. He said, "I'll be right next door if you need me, Mary."

"I think Mary has had more than enough help from you, Kelly Gantt. Now git."

Miss Hannah Wells was almost seventy years old, the local granny woman. She had delivered dozens of babies in this community. She was a large woman, but agile considering her size. She moved about the room with no missteps or mistakes. First, she filled two kettles from buckets of spring water on the washstand. The buckets of water were kept full at all times.

"If we need more, I'll send one of the gents in the next room to the kitchen house for it," Miss Hannah stated. "All they have to do is sit in front of their fire, probably having a swig of something for their anxiety. Huh! They don't have a clue when it comes to giving birth."

The kettles were placed on the wood stove and immediately began to sizzle from the touch of the hot cast iron. Kelly had built a good strong fire, and it wouldn't take long to heat the water.

Once the water was on the stove, Miss Hannah told Mary she needed to examine her in order to see how far along she was. She would then be able to tell how Mary's labor was progressing.

Mary understood the birthing process and trusted Miss Hannah's judgment, but the exam was still painful and embarrassing.

Not nearly as painful as the labor pains though, she had to admit to herself. And Kelly hadn't been far off base when he brought up the heifer comment; she just detested being compared to one of Mr. Kel's heifers.

"Since this is your first child, Mary, it may take its own good time getting here.

Do what I say, and don't worry about those fellows in the next room. If the pain gets too bad, you yell all you want to. It won't hurt a thing, and it may give you some relief.

I'll be right here to hold your hand and see that this baby comes into the world 'fine as a fiddle.' Do you understand, Mary? If you want to ask me anything, go right ahead. I've delivered dozens of babies; I'll try my best to explain."

"Why do you always boil so much water when babies come?" asked Mary between the contractions that were coming regularly now. Mary had never witnessed a woman giving birth. She'd always been relegated to some other room if a birth was in progress. Grown-ups had dismissed her, thinking her too young to witness a birth.

"Well, child, we'll need some way to sterilize those scissors when it comes time to cut the cord. Washing the little thing without some hot water to add to its bath would be plain stupid considering the condition of things: the cold. I mean. We don't want the baby to catch a chill. We'll also need some hot water to bathe and clean you up after the birth. A bit of warm water will make you feel better. We will get you and the baby all nice and cozy afterwards."

"OK, Miss Hannah, just tell me what to do, and I'll try my best."

The hours dragged by and the pains kept coming, Mary pushing when Miss Hannah told her. She tried not to scream when they hit. The pain began at the base of her spine and came around both sides of her belly, meeting in the middle in a crescendo of pure pain, a peak which seemed beyond endurance in intensity. It seemed almost impossible to Mary that the pain could be so intense. She just tried to keep her mind on what she would have when the pain was gone. It had been hours now, and Mary was beginning to show her exhaustion.

The kerosene lamp beside the bed made strange shadows on the ceiling. Mary watched them and tried to picture shapes in the shadows, just like with clouds in a blue sky. But her thoughts could not linger on anything tranquil when her body was in such turmoil.

"Scream all you want to, honey. Giving voice to pain may just help. Don't try to keep your feelings inside. Rant and rave against the injustice of a woman's lot. We women know what pain really is; think about the men-folks in the next room, sitting peacefully in front of the fire. Wouldn't you just love to scream at them for their indifference?"

Miss Hannah pulled back the cover to examine her patient once more. "Mary, I can see the baby's head. It won't be long now. Just push for me a couple more times, and this baby will be here."

* * * * *

Kelly had paced the floor in front of the fire until he had exhausted himself.

"Sit down, will you, Kelly, you're making us all nervous," said Sam. "No need to wear a path on the rug. Babies sometimes take their own sweet time getting here. That's what Ma says anyway. Me, I know nothing about delivering babies, just heifers."

"Don't even bring that up, will you, Sam? I tried to reassure Mary with the fact about birth being a natural thing on the farm. When I mentioned the heifers, she got right upset, said she wasn't a heifer. I dropped that line of logic like a hot potato. Hand me that bottle you have in your coat pocket, Roston. I think it might steady me some."

Roston produced the bottle, but before passing it over to Kelly, he took one long swig. "You know, this is pretty good stuff, if I must say so myself. We did a right good job in its production."

They passed around the bottle, each taking a long drink of the fiery liquid. "I'm beginning to really worry about Mary."

"Nonsense, Kelly, she'll be fine and so will that baby," said Roston.

Moans of pain continually reached their ears from the next room.

"I don't know about you two boys, but I need to get some fresh air," Kelly said. They all three got up, put on their coats, and went out on the front porch, closing the door behind them so as not to let out any of the precious heat. The rain had stopped, and a full moon shone from high overhead.

"It not as cold," said Sam. "This rain brought some heat back, I believe. It's probably close to 50 degrees." There were plenty of puddles in the yard and the air was heavy with dampness, but the temperature was up. It was well past midnight on Sunday morning, the sixteenth of October 1910: a quiet night. The three brothers sat silently, sipping whiskey to keep warm and waiting for a tiny baby to arrive.

"You boys can go on home if you want," said Kelly. He called them boys even though Roston was thirty-two, and Sam was twenty-two: both hardly boys. Both brothers were determined to keep Kelly company until the baby arrived.

They sat on the porch and talked in hushed voices. They talked about farming, their secret moonshine still, and of course about women. Roston and Sam did the talking about women; Kelly just nodded and smiled now and then. His mind was in turmoil with the same hesitant anxiety Mary was feeling, just without the unbearable pain that consumed her. All Kelly could think about was the event that was happening inside the house. A feeling of dread hung heavily over his head. He knew giving birth was not only painful but also dangerous; it was not uncommon for women to die in childbirth. His mind reeled with the possibility that he could lose Mary. He tried to push that devastating thought to the back of his mind, but no matter what, it kept slipping back.

* * * * *

"You're almost there, child, just one more hard push, and it'll be over."

When the intense pain cut through her body again, she bore down and pushed with all the strength she had left. It felt as though she was being ripped in two, but this time, the baby slipped out and the intensity of the pain immediately subsided.

The child let out a wail as Miss Hannah spanked his bottom. "It's a beautiful little boy, Mary, and he looks perfect to me."

"Hand him to me please, Miss Hannah," Mary said with out-stretched hands.

The sight of that tiny, precious being gave Mary a feeling of euphoria, coupled with an immediate maternal instinct so intense. At the sight of her son, so helpless and tiny, she would have glad-ly died for him then and there if need be. A mother's love is an indescribable feeling that overcomes all the pain that came before. The pain had disappeared, along with the memory of what agony it had been. The result, her baby, was worth every hurt she had endured.

"Just one minute, honey. I have to cut the cord and clean him up a bit." The baby began to whimper as Miss Hannah worked with him. "He's a little angel all right, and I know his daddy will be proud." She handed him to Mary and said, "We'll get you bathed and into a nice flannel gown. I'll strip this bed and put on clean sheets, then I'll just go and inform the fellows he's here and ready to be introduced to his daddy."

* * * * *

The men-folks, returning from the porch to the fire in the next room, already knew the baby was here: they had heard him wail as they entered. Kelly was beside himself with the need to go in and began the nervous pacing again.

"Calm down, Kelly, Miss Hannah will come and fetch you directly; she probably has some cleaning up to take care of," Roston said quietly.

The door opened and Miss Hannah appeared. "You can come in just a few minutes, Kelly, and meet your son."

"Hot damn! I just knew it would be a boy. Every man needs a son!" exclaimed Kelly.

Roston and Sam gave Kelly a congratulatory slap on the back as he left the room. "Don't go anywhere yet, fellows; I want you to meet your new nephew."

When Kelly entered the bedroom, Miss Hannah had Mary and the baby bathed and peacefully tucked in a clean bed. The soft glow from the kerosene lamp bathed their faces and they looked like angels to Kelly. Mary stirred as he drew near and Kelly could see the exhaustion on her face, but that baby was beautiful.

Mary smiled and said, "He looks like you I think."

"I'm sure I can't tell exactly who he looks like yet, Mary, but he sure looks like a Gantt to me," he said, with unmistakable pride in his voice. "Did you ever decide on what to call him? You remember I left that decision up to you."

"Yes, Kelly. I thought we would call him Leon Odell Gantt. I know it's not a family name; I just like the sound of it. Momma had a close cousin by the name Leon, and she spoke so highly of him. I thought it wouldn't hurt to give him a name of someone she dearly admired. The Odell part I came up with myself. I just thought the two names sounded fine together, that's all."

"Mighty high sounding name for such a little fellow, but its ok with me. Leon Odell Gantt," Kelly repeated. "I like it too, Mary. Well, Mr. Leon, welcome to the Gantt family."

* * * * *

A faint glow tinted the eastern sky as Roston and Sam headed back to Rayflin. A few clouds still lingered pink against the brightening sky.

"Kelly sure is proud of that boy," Roston said. "You would think he was the one that gave birth."

"Well I guess he did have a lot to do with it, Roston. I would sure be proud too."

"Wait 'til Ma and Pa finds out. Leon being their first grand-child, I'm sure they will be chomping at the bit to see him," replied Roston.

It wasn't much more than a mile to home and they rode the rest of the way in silence, both anticipating delivering the good news to the family.

The house at Rayflin sat near the road on a big curve, not two hundred yards from the North Edisto River.

Breaking the silence as they neared the final curve Roston re-marked, "Looking at this old house gives me a sense of belonging. Sam, can you remember what the original house looked like? You are quite a bit younger than me. You were just four or five when Pa decided we needed the addition built on. Jennie, Rion and Buck were not born until after the addition."

"I can barely remember what the original house looked like," Sam replied. "Ma has explained so many times what it was to be-gin with; maybe I just think I remember. It was five rooms with a staircase leading to a large room above under the slanted roof. A tall rock chimney rose on the outside of the end of the house nearest the road. That chimney still stands, along with the room that extended from rear of the house. Ma was so proud of the original, even though it was not a fancy house, and it was unpainted and very old.

"The original house was built long before the War Between the States and was made from hand-hewn pine lumber and put together with pegs and homemade pointed nails with hammered square heads. Of course, there was a separate kitchen out back, a precaution against fire, since meals were cooked over an open fireplace in those early years. Her description of course, not mine. Like I said, I'm not sure, it could just be a memory that she instilled so deeply in all of us growing up. It's more like a dream to me than something tangible I can vividly recall."

The house had been their mother Peninnah's home all her life, being the home of her grandparents, Russell and Elizabeth Gunter. These grandparents and her aunt, Merari Shaffer, had basically raised her. Both her parents died in 1864 when Peninnah was only four. Her mother, Ara, had died of pneumonia. Her father, Thomas Jefferson Woodward, a Confederate soldier, had died in that Yankee hellhole, Elmira Prison, in September of that year. Peninnah's grandparents, Russell and Elizabeth, had left their home to their daughter, Merari. After Peninnah married Kel Gantt, they had made their home here with Aunt Merari. Merari was called 'Auntie' by Peninnah and was looked upon as a mother, not just her mother's sister. Being only four years old when Ara died, Peninnah had few memories of her.

Kel and Peninnah had purchased the north section of two hundred fifty-seven acres from Aunt Merari and intended on building their home on their acreage.

"I would be pleased to leave the remaining two hundred fifty-seven acres to you both," Aunt Merari had suggested. "I only ask that you live here with me and see to my welfare. I am so lonesome living here alone. I'll deed the rest to you both, to be received at my death."

Kel and Peninnah had agreed without discussion. Aunt Merari was a loving old lady who considered her a daughter, since she and her German husband, Charles Shaffer, who had died years before, had no children. Aunt Merari had passed away earlier in 1910. Now the land was Kel and Peninnah's, free and clear.

Kelly and Mary's house was located on the north section of the property, part of which would belong to Kelly one day.

Kelly had often told Mary, "Pa, with the help of us boys and the hands working for him, increased the size of the house by three rooms in 1895. We painted the house at Rayflin white just two years back. It's now an old house haphazardly attached to Ma's original home."

* * * * *

Their parents were up and in the kitchen, now part of the main house, when Roston and Sam pulled in beside the house. "Well, Kel, I guess those boys of yours are back." She always called them 'his boys' when she suspected they had been into mischief.

Peninnah Gantt was a small woman, never weighing over a hundred pounds in her entire life, except for when she was expecting her babies. She had given birth to nine. Roston, the eldest, was thirty-two and Delmas—'Buck' he was called—was the baby, age ten. Between the two were Cyrus, Kelly, Corrie, Sam, Woodard, Jennie, and Rion. It was hard trying to raise seven boys. She always heard that girls were harder because they could get in the family way and cause disgrace to their parents. "Babies are a blessing but they should be legitimate as far as I am concerned," Peninnah would say, but she worried more over her boys. There was so much meanness around: fighting, thieving and even killing. But her biggest worry was the drinking. That usually led to one of the other evils. Only one of her boys, Kelly, and her daughter, Corrie, were married.

* * * * *

Sam and Roston eased across the front porch and opened the door as quietly as possible. The kitchen was two rooms straight back, and they could see their parents sitting at the kitchen table having breakfast. Peninnah leaned forward a bit from her side of the table and saw them sneaking in.

"Well, you boys needn't to be so quiet. We heard you drive in. I guess y'all have been out all night playing cards and drinking. Shame on you!"

"No, Ma, you've got that all wrong." Sam was the first to speak. "Actually, Ma, you might say we've been on an errand of mercy; we've been at Kelly's all night, keeping him company. Mary had her baby."

"Well, don't just stand there, get in here and tell us about it!" Peninnah waved them in excitedly.

"Come on, boys, and have some breakfast while you give us the news. Your Ma has a big pot of grits on the stove and some fried fatback."

Kel Gantt was excited too; you could hear it in his voice. This was their first grandchild, and he had been looking forward to having another baby around, just like Peninnah. Kel was a successful farmer; he relished the thought of grandchildren to leave this place to someday. He was not a tall man, barely five feet six inches; he was almost as big around as he was tall. Weighing over two hundred pounds, he was a barrel of a man, described as such by local menfolk based on his girth and height. He was often described as a keg with legs. Of course, this description was never mentioned in his presence, mind you. He sported a handlebar mustache and piercing blue eyes. He spoke with authority and on his land, his word was law.

"Well, it's a boy, and mother and baby are fine," said Roston. "They've named him Leon Odell, and according to Miss Hannah, he's about seven pounds. When we left, they were just fine. Kelly sure is proud of that boy."

"I just bet he is and rightly so. Proud as a peacock I was when you were born, Roston. That's not to say I wasn't proud of all my boys, and my girls too. It just seems having that first son is a mite special to a man, being such a new experience and all!" Kel exclaimed.

"Well, boys, as soon as you finish breakfast, we've got to get the stock fed. Your ma and I will be going up to Kelly's to see our grandson, and I'm sure y'all will be needing a little sleep."

* * * * *

Miss Hannah dozed in a chair beside the stove. She was as dedicated as any doctor and wasn't about to leave her patients until she knew everything was as it should be. She had helped Mary get the precious little boy to nurse the first time. He did fine and had been changed and tucked into the cradle Kelly made that sat beside the bed. It was well past sun up, and they both slept peacefully. Miss Hannah stirred from her nap to check once more on her patients.

"I'll be needing to get back home soon and check on that husband of mine," she said aloud to herself. She tiptoed into the next room to awaken Kelly. He passed out on the bed in the other room some two hours past. She shook him gently.

"Is everything OK, Miss Hannah?"

"Everything is fine with Mary and the baby. I just need to get on home now. Will your ma be coming up here to take care of things for a few days?"

"I'm sure her and Pa will be here directly. I'll just go harness the mule to the buggy and get you on home. Do you think it will be alright to leave Mary and the baby alone about thirty minutes?"

"They'll be fine for a little while. You just be sure she stays in that bed at least a week. Giving birth is hard on a woman, and she'll need time to get her strength back. I'll be down tomorrow afternoon to check on them."

"Don't worry about Mary and baby Leon. Mary is a strong woman, and I can depend on Ma to help us if need be. I appreciate all you did for Mary, helping her with the delivery. Lord knows I would have been completely lost if she didn't have you."

"Thank you for your confidence in me," Miss Hannah replied. "You would be amazed at the ungrateful people I have helped give birth. By the by, I do believe you and Mary will make wonderful parents. Just always remember, make your children behave, but love them, even when they disappoint. Love is an unconditional thing, no matter what."

"Thanks for taking care of Mary and for the advice," Kelly replied as he stretched out a hand with one gold coin in the palm.

Miss Hannah excepted the payment from Kelly reluctantly. "I wouldn't except this you know, Kelly, but we are not getting any younger, and my husband is in bad health. It's awfully kind of you to offer. I usually don't even get a thank you for my services."

"Well, you deserve this and so much more, that's a fact. I'll go fetch the buggy and get you home."

Three

DAYLIGHT WAS JUST BEGINNING TO CREEP IN THROUGH THE
bedroom windows when Mary awoke. Kelly was gone from their
bed, but the fire was going strong. A vague memory of the stove
door creaking open when Kelly had added more wood crossed her
mind. She had been in that state halfway between sleep and awake
where it is difficult to distinguish dream from reality. Slipping from
their bed, Mary padded silently across the wooden floor on bare
feet, avoiding that board underneath the rocker that squeaked with
the slightest pressure. She wanted to dress beside the fire before
Leon woke up again to be fed.

Mary nursed him once during the night. At half past two by the
mantle clock, she sat in the rocker beside the stove, feeding him at
her bosom and humming softly. When his diaper was changed, she
tucked him back into his cradle; he went right back to sleep.

So far, he has been a delightful baby, Mary thought to herself.
*At age four weeks, he only cries when he's hungry or needs his diaper
changed. Most of the time, he sleeps.*

She heard him stir in his cradle and begin to whimper. As she
bent over to pick him up, he yawned and stretched his little fists
over his head.

"You're ready for your breakfast, young man, aren't you?" His big brown eyes fastened on her face at the sound of her gentle question, softly cooing while she changed his wet diaper. Sitting beside the stove, she unbuttoned her blouse and nuzzled him to her bosom. Twenty minutes later, he'd had his fill. Mary sat him upright, leaning his little body over and supporting his chest. With her right hand, she patted and rubbed his back. He burped loudly. His little head drooped downward, and he drifted back to sleep.

Laying him back in his cradle, Mary whispered, "It's almost daylight, and I know your daddy will want his breakfast, too. You be a good boy, and I'll be back soon."

As Mary hurried out the back door toward the kitchen house, she caught a flurry of black and red from the corner of her eye. It was the old rooster lifting himself to his favorite perch on the lowest limb of the chinaberry tree. He began to crow loudly just as the sun crept above the pines to the east.

It's time for the day to begin and what a busy day it will be, she thought as she lifted the latch on the kitchen house door.

Kelly was sitting in front of the fireplace, gazing intently into the flames, a cup of steaming coffee in his right hand. He had built a fire for her in the wood cook stove and in the fireplace.

"My, that coffee sure smells good. Thank you for making a pot. I'll have your breakfast ready directly," she said, reaching upward to remove her bib apron from a nail beside the stove. Tying it securely in a bow, she asked, "What have you been doing all this time? I know you were up at least an hour."

"Well, I built the fires and made that pot of coffee on the stove; most of the time I've just been sitting here, spitting in the fire and waiting for the sun to come up. I've got to be getting down to

Rayflin pretty soon. I'm helping Pa and my brothers butcher those two hogs today. Pa expects the whole family to pitch in. This is one chore the boys won't be able to weasel out of; no slackers today. It's been mighty cold. That suits well for the butchering. It ain't warmed up above 40 degrees the last four days. That's perfect for hog killing; just the right temperature."

"You're right; it has been mighty cold lately. I'll get your breakfast ready so you can go on down to Rayflin."

"While you're cooking, I'll go out to the woodpile," Kelly said, standing and placing his cup on the mantle above the fire. "I know that wood box in our bedroom is getting pretty low. I'll fill it up and the big box on the porch. That way, you won't have to worry about keeping the fires going; there will be plenty of wood close at hand. When I get back this evening before dark, I'll fill them up again."

"Do the bedroom quietly. Leon is asleep and I would like for him to stay that way, at least until we're finished with breakfast. Why don't you just stack some on the front porch? I'll bring it inside after he wakes up. You might want to peep in on him before you go. Just tiptoe, okay?"

"I'd like to see the little fellow before I leave. I'll try to tiptoe, but I've never been a big tiptoer, as you well know," he said, laughing out loud as he headed for the woodpile. *Tiptoe, yeah right,* Kelly thought to himself. *Men don't tiptoe.*

Twenty minutes later, Mary and Kelly talked about the day's plans as they sat at the table, eating. The wood boxes had been filled, and Kelly managed to check on the baby without waking him. As they sat down for breakfast, he told Mary how Leon gave his daddy that sweet smile in his sleep.

"I've always heard when babies smile in their sleep, they're dreaming about angels," Mary said.

"I heard when babies smile in their sleep, they're just passing gas," Kelly replied.

"You always say the craziest things, Kelly," Mary said with the hint of a smile. "Now, to continue with our conversation about the work down at Rayflin, we both agree that the meat from the butchering will go a long way to help us make it through the winter. We don't have much money, of course."

Kelly reminded Mary, "I have my share of the cotton profits and the little money we make from our own acreage. Thank the good Lord we have land. There are many others not so lucky."

"Living in the country distant from the commerce of town life as we do, necessities are the only things that matter," Mary said. "Thankfully, most of those we either grow or raise here on the farm. We don't spend money on frivolous things. Of course, there are the needed staples: coffee, tea, sugar, and you men-folk have a need for your tobacco, but everything else comes from the farm. Grits, our main breakfast food, can be ground from our corn at the grist mill on Black Creek operated by Mr. Kel's brothers."

"It's a help to have my uncles grind our corn," Kelly remarked. "They always give Pa a cheaper price due to his being family and God knows, we eat a lot of grits."

Mary stood and began to clear the table, "I'm glad y'all are butchering those hogs today. Our salt pork is almost out, and the sausage and bacon have been gone a while. You need to get going, Kelly." After a brief pause, she added, "And don't forget to tell Miss Peninnah I'll be coming tomorrow to help with the sausage making and whatever else is left to do."

* * * * *

As soon as Kelly was out the door, Mary left the kitchen house and ran up the back steps to check on Leon. He was still sleeping peacefully and she didn't disturb him. *Maybe by the time you're crawling, son, it won't be so cold. Right now, I'm satisfied for you to sleep all the time. At least I can get my work done without worrying where you're at and what you're into,* Mary mentally noted.

* * * * *

Driving the farm wagon, Kelly passed the fork and started down the small rise in the sandy road within sight of Rayflin. He caught sight of the sun just peeping up above the pines to the east. Spotting his pa, Kel, and all the boys out near the barn, he steered the wagon in that direction.

They had separated the two hogs from the rest of the group and his pa had his rifle propped against his right shoulder. Just as Kelly pulled up in the wagon, he heard his pa's rifle fire once and then a second time. The hogs lay on their sides, dead; Kel was a good shot. He had hit them both in the perfect spot: the temple.

Now the real work could begin. Two huge iron pots of water boiled over fires behind the barn. Kel and Roston had gotten up long before daylight, filled the pots, and started fires underneath them so that by daybreak the water would be boiling hot.

The hogs were hung on a scaffold between two trees, their

throats were slit, and their bright red blood began to drain into tubs set on the ground beneath their carcasses. Time was allowed for all the blood to drain before the next step began. Sam and Woodard then removed the tubs from under both hogs, dumping the blood in a hole dug at the edge of the woods. Roston and Kelly, using boards, strained to pick up the huge pots of steaming water. They had to be particular: they didn't want to slosh any of the boiling water on the ground or on themselves. They carefully poured the steaming water into a large oak barrel that lay at a 45-degree angle in a slanted hole in the ground. Sam and Woodard removed the first hog from the scaffold and carried it over to the barrel in the ground. They submerged the rear half of the animal into the hot water, then switched ends and dunked the front half. The timing of the dunking had to be precise, too long in the boiling water, and the hair would be set, making it almost impossible to remove with the scrapping. The hog was then placed on a burlap cotton sheet spread out under an oak beside the barn.

The hair was scraped off by Roston and Kelly with a scrapping tool. While they started removing the hair on the first hog, Woodard and Sam submerged the second animal. When both hogs had been submerged in the hot water and placed on the cotton sheet, everyone pitched in to clean them, except for Rion and Buck. They were present but too young to be trusted with sharp scrapping knives or pouring boiling water. They had other jobs, washing all the hair off the carcasses and cleaning the hogs' feet, things they could be trusted with. By the time the animals were cleaned and ready to hang, it was near eleven o'clock, almost time for dinner. The animals needed to hang a while before the actual butchering began so that the meat could firm up in the cold air.

They knew Peninnah would ring their dinner bell when dinner was on the table; they had a few minutes to sit in the bright sunlight, where the temperature was more comfortable, and rest and smoke or chew tobacco, which Kel preferred. "We at least get a few minutes to catch our wind before dinner," Kel said. "I'm sure glad I have you boys to do the heavy work. I'm not a young buck anymore in case y'all haven't noticed." His sons said nothing, just smiled.

Roston held a hand beside his mouth and whispered in secretive fashion to the others, "We all know Pa can still whip our ass if he had a mind to." The other brothers just nodded in agreement when their pa wasn't looking.

* * * * *

Peninnah and Jennie, her fifteen-year-old daughter, had been busy all morning, cooking dinner and getting everything ready to help process the butchered hogs afterwards. A big pot of turnip greens and a pan of cornbread sat on the back of the cook stove, ready for the hungry men.

Peninnah had sent Jennie out to the back yard two hours earlier. "Dig us up a passel of sweet potatoes, about ten or so, from the bank in the backyard, and we'll wash them good and cook them with cinnamon and nutmeg. You know how much your pa loves sweet potatoes." For dessert, they had fried apple pies using the dried apples from last fall's harvest. Peninnah and Jennie had worked hard too. They knew the men-folk would need a good meal to sustain them through the busy afternoon.

At 11:45, everything was ready. The table was set and the food placed in the center, covered to keep warm.

"Please, Ma, may I ring the dinner bell?" Jennie asked.

"Go ahead," Peninnah replied. "I knew you would want to."

Jennie ran outside to the back porch, where a triangle of iron dangled on a heavy chain from the eaves of the porch. She had brought one of Peninnah's large metal spoons from the kitchen and hit the inside of the iron triangle on all sides. With the heavy metal spoon, Jennie felt the vibration clean up to her shoulder. The loud waves of sound were almost deafening. Heavy metal-on-metal clanging reverberated through the air.

The table was set for the men-folk to eat their noon meal, and they were soon there. They tromped up the back steps to the porch, stopped long enough to pour water from a bucket into the pan and wash their hands. They all knew this was one of Peninnah's strictest rules. "Wash your hands or don't eat," she would always remind them. Pulling their chairs out, they plopped down. Pausing with bowed heads just long enough for Kel to say grace, they devoured the food with relish. Banter was light; they were more concerned with eating than small talk. The cold weather, squirrel hunting and the latest goings-on down the road in Sugar Bottom were mentioned, but only briefly. Eating their delicious dinner far outweighed talking. Peninnah was a good cook. No way could conversation minimize turnip greens, cornbread, sweet potatoes, and fried apple pies. They knew once the meal was over, there would be no leisure time for any of them. They enjoyed their food, the company of family, and the talk, especially the gossip about their neighbors. They soon finished and reluctantly returned to their chore of butchering up at the barn.

Peninnah and Jennie put away the food and washed dishes while the men went back to their work.

The hogs were butchered; first they were split down their abdomen with a sharp long knife, cutting through the outside layers of thick skin. Their insides fell into the clean tubs placed under each hanging animal.

"Lord Almighty!" Rion exclaimed, witnessing the insides tumbling into the tub. "I thought hogs smelled bad on the outside—their guts smell even worse."

"Watch the way you use God's name, boy," his pa said. "You may as well get used to the smell. Wait until you're emptying the intestines and cleaning them—that's a smell you won't be forgetting any time soon. It has to be done, and don't you and Buck start puking. You'll not get out of that job."

Most of the animal's organs would be used. The intestines would be cleaned for casings to stuff the ground sausage into. Cleaning the casings fell to Buck and Rion, the youngest boys, age ten and twelve. This was the first time they had been awarded this chore, and they were not pleased. Of course, they would need supervision; no one volunteered for this job, so they drew straws. Sam got the short one.

"Cleaning the entrails is bad enough," Sam said, "but supervising these two nitwits to make sure they do a decent job is a close second."

The saying among farmers was, 'Nothing on a hog wasted except for the squeal.' The meat was cut up on a long table near the barn and piled in dishpans to be carried to the kitchen.

A separate table was devoted to cleaning the intestines. They had to be turned inside out and all the contents squeezed out into a hole near the tree line. Then the emptied casings were washed in a pan of clean water until all the disgusting residue was gone; this washing had to be repeated several times with fresh water until they were clean to Sam's satisfaction.

Meanwhile, Peninnah and Jennie removed the oilcloth from the kitchen table and scrubbed the table down with lye soap and hot water boiled on the wood cook stove. As the men brought in the meat, the women trimmed it, salted it down and packed it in oak barrels. The trimmings would be ground up for sausage. The fat from the hogs was put in a big iron pot over a fire out back and melted for lard. They all worked hard through the afternoon and by five p.m., things were in pretty good shape. The meat was salted down and packed away, the hams were soaking in brine to be hung later in the smokehouse, and the trim meat was covered with cheesecloth to be seasoned, ground, and packed in the cleaned casings the next day. The weather was so cold, they could wait to make the sausage. It would be fine on the back porch, sealed up so no varmints could get to it.

Back up at the barn, Kel and the boys put things away and emptied and washed the dishpans, dumping any leftover water from the cast iron pots.

"Well, Pa, I'll be going on home now," Kelly said. "Mary will be coming in the morning to help with the sausage making. When that's done and we get the hams and sausage hanging in the smokehouse, we'll be all set for meat this winter."

"I thought we might butcher two or three more of my hogs while the weather is right," Kel suggested. "What do you and the boys think?" he said, directing his question to the whole brood beside the barn. "My Farmer's Almanac is forecasting a hard winter; can't be a bad thing to be prepared."

"That sounds like a fine idea," Kelly said, his brothers nodding in agreement. "You just pick the time, Pa, and we'll get it done."

Kel's sons knew it was not wise to disagree with him when it came to the workings of the farm. Kel was a smart man and he considered the Farmer's Almanac only one step below the Bible and the major authority concerning the weather and time for planting his acreage.

"Kelly, you go ahead and take a barrel of that salted pork up to your house tonight if you want to. That will still leave three barrels here. If we do more butchering, there will be plenty for the whole family all winter, and when the sausage and the hams are cured, y'all can have some of that meat too."

"Thanks, Pa," Kelly said, stepping onto the wagon wheel, boosting himself onto to the bench seat, and grabbing the reins. "We'll be here bright and early in the morning." Sam was thinking, *Kelly gets to go home for the night while the rest of us are stuck here with Pa rehashing our performance today.* Kel was never very liberal when it came to praise; there was always something that they could have done better, and he was pretty sure cleaning the casings with Buck and Rion would not be to their pa's liking. He was so damned critical, everything had to be done his way. Sam envied Kelly being able to escape the criticism he knew was coming.

* * * * *

Mary had their supper cooked and the table set when Kelly came in the kitchen house door. She had brought little Leon out to the kitchen and made a pallet for him in front of the fire. He was awake for a change and lay there, quite content, watching the fire, waving his little fists and kicking his feet inside his drawstring gown.

"How did everything go with the butchering?" Mary asked.

"Just fine. We finished everything except for the sausage grinding. I told Pa and Ma we would be there early in the morning to finish up. Pa suggests while the weather is right we might as well butcher some more animals. That way, none of us will run low on meat this winter."

"That's good to hear, Kelly. Your pa must think we're in for a hard winter; he's real knowledgeable when it comes to such things. I guess as soon as we eat and I get things cleaned up in here, we need to get to bed. I'll have to get up at least once to feed Leon. He is a good little boy though: just sleeps and eats mostly."

"I'll remind you about that 'good boy' part in a couple of years. He's a Gantt, ain't he? Bound to get into mischief, I think. Ma always said we were such sweet babies, and then we grew up and turned mean. She didn't say we were mean as in treated people badly for no reason; some of us just naturally didn't take too well to people telling us what to do or trying to push us or other defenseless people around. Nothing makes me angrier, even when I'm sober, than some braggart talking hateful to old people or little children. Sam is the same way, and I think Buck will be too. He's only ten, but I can already see he always takes up for the underdog."

Kelly continued, "As for as Sam, don't get him riled up. He has a long memory and thinks he is invincible. I think he believes he could walk into a circle saw and not get cut, especially when he's had a snoot full. It's best not to mess with us in that kind of situation. Otherwise we are gentle as lambs. Wouldn't you agree, Mary?"

"I wouldn't go so far as to use 'gentle as lambs,' but I do understand what you're saying. I'm hoping Leon takes more after me in his disposition, although you have been a wonderful husband and father so far. I must remember not to get you 'riled up' by picking on the defenseless."

"You, my sweet wife, have nothing to worry about. You're more of a push-over, willing to help anyone who asks. The whole family loves you, black and white, on this farm. Now, I think you're right; we need to get some rest. Busy day tomorrow."

Four

MORNING CAME SOON ENOUGH AND MARY, KELLY, AND BABY Leon headed down to Rayflin. They took the buggy since it was more comfortable for Mary and the baby. This was his first trip away from home, and Mary was so afraid to take him out. He was still so tiny and the weather had been so cold. But this morning, he was bundled in blankets and there was no way he could feel the chill of the morning air.

It was just daylight when they arrived at Rayflin. Kelly pulled the buggy into the space beside his pa's Model T, underneath the big magnolia tree in the front yard. After taking Leon, Kelly waited for Mary to climb down.

"Give him to me, Kelly," Mary said. "I can carry him up the steps if you could just get his diaper bag from under the seat."

Once Mary was in the house, Kelly headed up to the barn with the men-folk.

Penninah was so pleased to see Leon again and wanted to hold him for a few minutes before the sausage-making got underway. They made Leon a pallet away from the fireplace and set to work.

The trimmed meat was ground up with a sausage grinder mounted on the corner of the cook table. It was seasoned with salt, pepper, a little cayenne, and lots of sage. After the women had it mixed, they fried some patties to be sure the taste was right. Then it was all stuffed into the cleaned casings to be smoked, along with the hams, in the smoke house out back. After the sausage had been smoked a couple of weeks, Peninnah would cut the sausage into links, stuff them in glass jars, and pour melted hog lard over them to seal them up. The sausage would last longer that way.

It was just the way Peninnah had been taught when she was growing up. Her grandma had done it that way, and all that grease certainly did not seem to have any adverse effect on either of her Gunter grandparents. Her grandma lived to the age of ninety-five and her grandpa to ninety-eight.

Stuffing the ground meat into the casings was pretty much an all-day job. At dinner time, Peninnah fixed sausage biscuits for the men-folk and a gallon of sweet tea for Jennie to deliver up at the barn, along with some clean rags and a bar of octagon soap

"Tell your pa, I hope they all have the good sense to wash their hands before they eat," Peninnah reminded Jennie.

The men-folk were too busy cleaning up their mess from the butchering and only took a break to sit under the oak tree and eat the food Jennie brought to them. Kel insisted everything used in the butchering process be cleaned and put away. He was not an easy man to please when it came to the condition of his barn and all his farm implements. All the sharp knives and scraping tools had to be washed and sharpened, hung in a particular section of barn, away from all the gear for the mules, the plow lines, and Kel's blacksmithing tools. Everything had its place and that's where Kel intended it to be.

While Mary and Jennie finished up with the sausage stuffing,

Penninah cooked a big pot of dried beans and cornbread for their supper. Of course, they took turns checking on baby Leon on his pallet, who was mostly sleeping the day away. He did wake up to be fed by his mother and have his diaper changed. Otherwise they hardly knew he was there; he was such a "good boy," like his mother had said the night before.

Kelly and Mary stayed for supper with the family before heading home.

Leon lay sleeping in Mary's arms, oblivious to the bumpy road. Mary and Kelly carried on a quiet conversation all the way there.

"I am so glad the butchering is finished, at least until Pa decides on having another one," Kelly said. "That is sure a hard job, especially with Pa in charge; everything has to be done according to his way of thinking. Of course, I have to admit, Pa is an expert, but he doesn't put up with shirkers."

"That's understandable, Kelly. He expects his boys to do things the right way," Mary said quietly. "Your pa is the very best at running a farm in these parts, and he does know best."

"Of course he does, but I wish you could have seen the look on his face when the hog was split and all the organs tumbled in the tub underneath. It was just priceless when Rion commented on how bad the insides smelled. I thought for sure Pa was going to cuff his ears." Remembering the moment, Kelly smiled to himself.

"Why was your pa so upset about that?" Mary asked.

"Never mind, Mary. I guess you just had to be there to witness their exchange to appreciate the humor."

Darkness had barely settled over the land when they reached home. Kelly immediately got the fire going in their bedroom. While Mary fed Leon, Kelly went to the barn to feed the stock. When he returned, Leon was already tucked into the cradle. Mary and Kelly sat a spell beside the potbellied stove in their bedroom, talking about their day and how tried they were; soon, they decided to turn in themselves.

* * * * *

On the twelfth of December, Mary and Leon accompanied Kelly for a visit at Rayflin. Miss Peninnah and Jennie were busy making their traditional fruitcake, so Mary pitched in to help with the preparation.

While the fruitcake was baking, the women-folk sat in the front room playing with Leon and discussing their Christmas plans.

"I'm sure sorry, Miss Penninah, that we won't be here for Christmas. Kelly, Leon and I will be going to Batesburg to visit my pa and will be staying with my sister Peggy and her husband Tom. I hope that isn't too disappointing for you," Mary said.

"Don't worry about disappointing us, child. If you have a chance to visit with your family, I'm pleased. I know how it is when we get busy with our lives and don't get to see everyone on holidays. Just be sure and take your family some of my fruitcake and wish them all a Merry Christmas from us."

"Thank you for understanding. I'll be sure and do that."

While the women were baking and visiting, the men were busy outside with the livestock and repairs to equipment and such. The mule lot needed some repair work before the mules were moved there for the winter.

"They should have already been moved from the upper pasture," Kel told his sons. "Farming is serious business if done right, and keeping the mules up in the pasture this late in the year is not a good idea." I don't care what people hereabouts say, there are still cougars and wolves down in the swamp, believe it or not. I've heard them on cold winter nights, and they could get into that upper pasture and kill one of my mules before they could be stopped. During the winter months, my mules can't forage for much in the pastures, so they need to be kept close to home."

There was corn in the corncrib and the fodder pulled and bundled as soon as the corn dried in the fields. The fodder bundles and corn were fed to the mules in the winter. Bales of straw cut and bundled were used as bedding for the animals that lived in the barn when the weather was extremely cold or rainy. Most days, weather permitting, they were released into the big lot attached to the barn.

Kelly and four of his brothers, Woodard, Sam, Rion, and Buck, were helping their father this December day, but Roston was not present. Cyrus was way off in Alabama managing a Turpentine Still, away from the farm for good, Kel figured.

"And just where is Roston today, Pa?" Kelly asked.

"Oh, he's out there in the storehouse trying to get everything set up for business. He's been busy making a list of supplies to order from Parler & Son Distributors in Batesburg to stock the store. He thinks he can make a go of being a store proprietor. I'm not at all sure about that, but we'll see. Wants to send his order by the train this evening, I believe he said."

* * * * *

The storehouse had sat behind Kel and Peninnah's house for years. Kel had even run the place once as a store, but with the farm, he didn't have much time to devote to the business. At that time, his sons were all too young and wild, and he couldn't trust them with any venture involving money. The building had sat idle for several years and now Roston had decided to try his hand as a storekeeper. They had moved the store building across the road and the railroad tracks just last spring and turned it to face the opposite direction. To accomplish this task, it had taken several days and the help of a stump puller. The building had sat high off the ground in front and low in the back before it was moved. At its present location, the front door was just one step up from the ground and the back of the building was four feet high. The store was one room, twenty feet by forty, with counters on both sides and shelves lining the walls.

"After we're finished up here, Pa, I might go on down that way and see if I can help Roston out with his order," said Kelly.

* * * * *

When Kelly stepped inside the storehouse door, it was dark except for one kerosene lamp on the counter. Roston was hunched over some papers with pencil in hand, working on his list of goods for the store. The counters were dusty and all the shelves were empty.

"Pa told me I would find you here, Roston. How is that list coming along?"

Pausing, his pencil in midair, Roston looked up at his brother to reply.

"I'm sure going to need a lot of stock to get this place going again. Pa has agreed to help finance the initial order for the goods if I can turn a profit and pay him back in six months. He says I need to do something constructive so that I can afford a wife and family in the near future. Says I'll need something to bring in some money besides just helping with the farming. You could help me run this place, Kelly. You've always been good with figures. I could sure use someone to help keep the books and free me up for some courting time. If I'm to please Pa, I best better start working on that wife and young'uns."

"Well, Roston, I'll sure give it some thought. Mary and I could use a little extra cash, and I've been hankering to buy an automobile of my own, but don't mention that to Mary."

"No problem. I know it would be nice to have your own automobile and not have to borrow Pa's. Course, the roads around hereabouts are just sand beds. It's a heap more convenient to just ride the train. That reminds me, if I'm going to get this order sent out today, I'd better finish up. It's nigh on to 2:00; the 'Swamp Rabbit' will be leaving Batesburg on the way to Perry. I've got to have this list ready when she comes back by on the return trip. How about you give me some ideas as to the inventory I'll need. I'll make the list, you just tell me what to put on it, deal?"

"Sure, Roston, I'll tell you what things you'll be needing on your list and you can write them down. Your time is getting short. The 'Swamp Rabbit' will be barreling down that track, smoke stack puffing, gray smoke bellowing to the tops of the trees and whistle screeching in less than two hours," he said, adding in a cautionary tone, "Of course, there's always the possibility she might be early."

"How well I know and I've got to be on the track signaling the

48

engineer as soon as she rounds the bend from Sugar Bottom. She can't stop on a dime, you know, and boy, the sparks will be flying."

"We better get on with that list, Roston. I'll dictate and you put it down."

"Ready when you are, Kelly."

"Well, let's see. We need to keep in mind what will be necessary for the local customers. We need some canned goods, sugar, coffee, flour, and salted meats. Also, good scales for weighing the sugar, coffee, and meat, since it will be bought in bulk, not pre-packaged. The flour will be sold in twenty-five pound bags. We'll need a good many bags of flour, say twenty-five to start. Every woman I know uses a goodly amount of flour: biscuits or hoe cakes are a necessity at every meal. You also need turpentine, castor oil, and medicines along with hardware, overalls, work boots, some bolts of piece goods, and a small selection of ready-made clothing items for the ladies. One important item is chewing tobacco and some Prince Albert's loose tobacco in cans for those fellows that roll their cigarettes. Might be a good idea to order at least a half dozen pre-packaged cigarettes—those with the three ones are real popular, put them on your list."

"Slow down a little, Kelly. I can't keep up and I'm going to have to use my pocket knife and trim this damn pencil here shortly. Take a breather and just think while I do that, ok?"

* * * * *

"Lordy! I believe I hear the 'Swamp Rabbit' coming from Batesburg heading on to Perry," Kelly said, cocking his head to one side.

Five minutes later, the sound of the iron wheels on the rails was unmistakable, and then the conductor blew the whistle in salute as she careened past, not twenty yards from the store building where Roston and Kelly stood.

The train that passed through Rayflin, a connecting line between Batesburg and Perry, was referred to as 'the Swamp Rabbit.' No one was sure how it got that name. It traveled at the exorbitantly high speed of fifteen miles per hour and it followed the North Edisto river swamp most of the way. Perhaps it was the speed, fast as a rabbit, and the terrain it traveled through that gave some bright soul the idea. The spur line that ran through Rayflin between Batesburg and Perry was built in 1898 and its completion was a major occasion. The hard-working people living near the track felt a connection to the rest of the world at simply knowing the 'Swamp Rabbit' could transport them to busy towns and cities. Places where there were electric street lights, street cars, and stores filled with all manner of modern conveniences and fancy clothes that could be purchased. Sometimes just hearing the whistle and feeling the rumble of the passing train would transport their minds to another place, somewhere far away from the toil and struggle of their mundane existence. Riding the rails was wishful thinking, but it gave them pleasure to imagine.

It was almost 3:30 when Roston was finally satisfied with the list he had made. Kelly had stayed, giving Roston ideas as to what was necessary for the local customers.

"Well, how about some of those bottled co-colas? We have that ice box up front we can keep them cold in as long as we have ice," Roston suggested. "The Swamp Rabbit can bring ice from town every other day or so."

"That sounds real good, Roston. You know, business might be pretty good with those fellows from over at the chalk mine that come by here in the evenings. That is, if they don't spend all their pay at the company store."

"And I figure we'll have all those folks from down in Sugar Bottom that will trade here, and the folks that live around Pine Grove church," Roston replied. "This will be a heap closer than going to Steadman or Batesburg for the necessities. And most of the boys here about will be stopping by for a little gossip, visiting, and a sociable drink. I'll have my jug under the counter for special visitors only. Just hope Pa don't find out."

"Well, Roston, I won't be telling him. But you can bet all the boys hereabouts will bring their own when they stop by. Booze is easy to come by in Sugar Bottom. You know, in that neck of the woods, it's hard to find someone to sell your liquor to. Most everybody makes their own."

"Not me. Sam was in charge of that still we had on Pelt Branch, but I think he has about given it up for now. Too afraid the law will find it, I guess, or maybe Pa. That would be worse."

"Pa can be right contrary when it comes to running moonshine stills on his land." Kelly laughed. "He doesn't mind having a drink once in a while, but it sure better be legal liquor!"

"You're right about that, Kelly. By the way, have you heard? Ma got a postcard this morning from Cyrus in Alabama. Says everything is going well with the turpentine still he's running for that big timber concern out there. He has three white fellows working for him now and about twenty-five blacks."

* * * * *

"I need to write a letter to Cyrus and tell him about his new nephew, Leon, and about this new business venture of ours," said Kelly.

"So you have decided to help me run the store, little brother," Roston said with a twinkle in his eye. He knew Kelly couldn't resist when it came to socializing with the local fellows. To Roston. the social aspect of running a business was his top priority. He was the most sociable of Kel and Peninnah's boys. He was easy-going and loved to talk to people and tease those he knew could take it *and* those that couldn't. He was well-liked and not as easy to get riled as Sam, Kelly or Buck. He loved to gossip and at times, his gift of gab got him into lots of trouble. Kelly always said, "Roston just does not know when to keep his mouth shut and sometimes it leads to him getting himself into tight spots."

"I guess I'd better help you with the business, or you'll lose your shirt," replied Kelly. "We can't be extending credit to all the folks around here, only a select few. I will decide who. Is that understood? That's the terms if I'm going to be keeping the books."

"Sounds fair enough to me," said Roston.

Truth be known, the socializing was a big a part of Kelly's decision to join Roston in his store venture as well. People who worked so hard to survive didn't have time to visit except if they had goods to buy or a death to mourn. Both occasions often involved the necessity of a little libation tucked in the participant's coat pocket. Especially in these desperate times, all the Gantt brothers and their neighbors drank strong spirits whenever they were with others, no matter the circumstance.

People in the South set great store in respect of the dearly departed. Friends and family would gather at the deceased's home, bringing food to sustain the survivors and saying how good the deceased looked all 'laid out.' The coffin usually sat in the parlor in front of a window and several friends felt it was their duty to sit up all night with the deceased. Why they did this no one could really say. No one was about to steal the body; maybe none of the family could rest with a body in the front parlor. There was also the uncertainty in the early part of the 20th century that the deceased was actually dead. Embalming was not the norm at that time with country folks. They didn't have the luxury of mourning their loved ones for too long; they had to get on with the business of surviving. It was sometimes expedient to get the burial over quickly. Or just maybe it was a Southern tradition, and you just didn't mess with the way things are done in the South.

"Well, I guess I best be heading on to the house," Kelly said, heading out the door. "I'll see you in a couple of days," he tossed over his shoulder, and was gone.

Five

KELLY STEPPED FROM BENEATH THE ROOF OF RAYFLIN'S RAIL-
road shack into the bright sunshine. It was Saturday, the twen-
ty-fourth of December, almost half past 11:00 and time for the
'Swamp Rabbit' to be passing through on the way to Batesburg.
From where Kelly stood, he could see way down the track to the
south; the train would blow her whistle when she crossed the river
trestle, which would allow plenty of time for him to fetch Mary and
the baby from Ma's. Kel and Peninnah's house stood behind him
and across the road about 100 feet away.

The railroad shack was nothing but a covered waiting shed for
passengers, built to protect them from the elements. It was 12 by
16 feet with no floor, boarded on two sides halfway vertically and
across the back for the entire 16 feet. On the back wall was a long
bench where passengers could wait, and if they stepped to the front
of the shelter, they could look left and right down the tracks.

Suddenly, Kelly heard a train whistle blow to the south. *She's
crossing the River Trestle*, he thought. *Better go get Mary and Leon.*

As he turned towards the house, Mary appeared on the front
porch holding Leon. Peninnah was behind her, carrying a basket.
Probably some of that dang fruitcake, he thought.

"I'll take that basket, Ma," he said as he stepped up on the porch. "We better hurry, Mary; I have to flag the train."

"Where are our traveling bags—Kelly and Leon's things?"

"They're on the bench in the railroad shack. Won't take but a minute to fetch them when the train comes to a stop."

As they reached the railroad shack, Kelly's whole being absorbed the scream of the train whistle and the bellowing smoke from the engine's stack. Trains were a marvel to him, a vision of things to come. No matter if the train was waved down for passengers or not, the engineer always gave a little salute with the whistle when passing through Rayflin.

When the train came into view, Kelly stepped onto the tracks and waved his arms so that the engineer would know there were passengers waiting to board. The whistle blew again, along with a loud deafening screech, giving Leon a start. He began to cry and his mother tried to calm him. When the train applied her brakes and came to a stop in front of the railroad shack, sparks were flying from the iron wheels. Kelly knew the engineer, Smoke Thompson, and the conductor, Howard Chapman.

Although this was not a scheduled stop, they frequently delivered parcels and picked up and dropped off passengers at Rayflin. Now, with Roston's store business, the train would be delivering goods on a regular basis.

The conductor, Howard Chapman, stepped from the train to welcome them aboard. "Kelly, are you folks heading to Batesburg today to visit the family?"

"Sure are, Howard, going to Mary's folks for Christmas."

"The fare is seventy cents Kelly, for you and Mary. The baby rides free," said Chapman.

Kelly paid their fare and they climbed aboard the passenger car.

After the initial shock of the train whistle, Leon calmed down and seemed to enjoy the train's rocking motion. Because of the cold of December, all the windows in the passenger car were raised, saving those inside from the smoke, soot and any wayward sparks. There was a small wood heater at the front of the passenger car, but it really did not furnish very much heat; passengers had the good sense to bundle up and carry a blanket.

The three settled onto a leather bench, placing their belongings in the seat facing theirs. Mary spread their blanket over their lower bodies and little Leon was snuggled down between his parents. This made a relatively cozy little nest for the trip to Batesburg.

* * * * *

The train finally pulled into the depot at Batesburg at fifteen minutes after noon. Tom Shealy was waiting at the depot to transport the Gantts to their home.

As Tom reached for Mary's hand to help steady her as she stepped down from the train, he said, "I apologize, Mary, but Peggy said she just could not leave our ham in the oven, but she can't wait to see you, Kelly, and most of all that bright-eyed little baby. My car is right near; we'll be there in no time."

They pulled into the Shealy's driveway within twenty minutes. Peggy rushed off the porch to greet her sister and brother-in-law, but most of all, she wanted to hold the baby. Peggy had no children of her own and so longed for a child.

"He is absolutely beautiful," Peggy said as she lifted him from Mary's arms. "I am so glad y'all agreed to come. We are truly happy to have the company, and Papa Fink can't wait to see his new grandson. He's waiting in the parlor; the weather is so cold he has to stay near the fireplace. Rheumatism I believe."

Papa Fink was truly pleased to see Mary, Kelly, and his baby grandson. Placing Leon on his Grandpa Fink's lap, Peggy remarked, "Isn't he a beautiful baby, Papa?"

"He sure enough is," replied Grandpa Fink. The old man's eyes fairly twinkled with pleasure holding the precious little boy, his first grandchild.

The rest of the afternoon was spent catching up on each other's lives, with Mary and Peggy in the kitchen preparing for the Christmas feast, Leon in his cradle for his afternoon nap, and the men-folk in the parlor talking and smoking cigars. They even drank a cup or two of Peggy's eggnog with some of Tom's fine brandy to add extra flavor.

It was a leisurely afternoon, at least for the men-folk. Mary and Peggy were working in the kitchen, but being together, talking and laughing, dismissed any thoughts of work from their minds. Their time together was the most important.

* * * * *

Christmas morning dawned clear and cold. There was a little breeze from the north and the few remaining leaves on the oak trees in Peggy's front yard twisted and danced in the cold air. Mary touched the windowpane and felt the cold as she bent over to pick Leon up and headed for the kitchen.

"I'm sorry I wasn't up earlier," Mary said as she entered the kitchen, seeing Peggy busy at the stove.

"Don't worry about the time; it's only half past 7:00. The men have already had their breakfast and are out back talking about Tom's new automobile. They are just itching to go for a ride, but I told Tom not today. It's Christmas and we're going to spend the day together. All men are the same," said Peggy. "We do all the work and they just stand around talking about what needs to be done. I'll fix you some breakfast while you nurse Leon and we can talk some more."

The two sisters enjoyed just being together again, laughing, talking, and sharing memories from their childhood. They hadn't been together in a while, and they didn't run out of stories to share all morning.

At precisely 12:30, the two sisters set the table for Christmas dinner. Peggy's table was 'a beauty' to behold. She had the loveliest china, crystal tea goblets and silverware placed on a white cutwork tablecloth with napkins to match. The centerpiece was a beautiful poinsettia that Tom had purchased.

"I'm sure glad Leon is just a baby, or I would fear for your fine dinnerware and crystal," Mary stated.

"It wouldn't bother me one iota if a piece of my fine china or crystal got broken. They are only material things. They don't mean anything unless their beauty can be shared with family. Remember that, Mary," Peggy replied. "I won't be taking any of these things with me; in the end, family and beautiful memories are what matters. If something is broken or accidentally spilled, it would only make Christmas more memorable I'm sure."

When everything was ready, the table set and the food on the table, Peggy called the men-folk to come in. "Christmas dinner is ready to be served, and I mean now." She added the last part firmly, so as not to be put off and to let the men in the back yard know she was not to be ignored. "Funny, Papa's rheumatism doesn't seem to be bothering him outside in the cold. Maybe they've already been into Tom's brandy."

Tom sat at the head of the table with Peggy to his right and his father-in-law, Mr. Fink, to his left. After grace was said, he carved the ham and placed some on each person's plate as it was passed to him. The dinner was delicious and followed by several desserts, including Miss Peninnah's fruit cake. They had coffee with their dessert. Then the men retired to the parlor for a cup of eggnog with Tom's imported brandy. They didn't hint that they had already had some of that fine brandy, and Peggy never mentioned it. After all, it was Christmas; she didn't want to start a fuss. Peggy and Mary cleaned off the table and put away the food, then joined the men in the parlor.

They sang Christmas carols together and Papa Fink talked about Christmas when he was a boy, back before he served in the War as a Confederate Soldier. "During the war years, Christmases were depressing and bleak," he said, only stating the obvious. Why tell what he witnessed: all the death, destruction and starvation. Christmas was, he thought, the time for good memories, not bad.

After sharing a quiet supper of leftovers with Peggy and Tom, all turned in to get some rest.

As they lay in bed that night, Kelly said, "You're right, Mary. Tom and Peggy were happy to see us. Tom was not at all what I expected.

He was easy to talk to and genuinely interested in what I had to say. I really do like Tom Shealy, and I respect him."

"It's wonderful to hear you say that, Kelly. You know how close I am to my sister. I'm really pleased you have enjoyed the visit. Now, we better get to sleep—we have an early train to catch."

Six

SPRING HAD COME TO SOUTH CAROLINA AT LONG LAST. MID-March signaled the beginning of planting season, and Kelly was busy from daylight to dark helping his pa at Rayflin while planting his own fields. The corn had to be sown by March twentieth. That was one of Mr. Kel's strictest rules. He put in his crops according to the phases of the moon and the Farmer's Almanac.

Evenings for Kelly were spent helping Roston in the store. Mary filled her days and evenings cooking, cleaning, and tending to Leon. He could turn over, sit up by himself, and was beginning to crawl. He was definitely developing his own little personality. He was a happy baby, always smiling and clinging to his momma.

On occasion, Mary could see Leon was indeed his father's child. He could be contrary when things didn't go his way, refusing to open his mouth when she tried to feed him grits from the table. He would clamp his little lips shut and turn his head, ignoring his mother's admonition to open and eat his food like a good little boy.

"I think his daddy jinxed his behavior when he said that good little boy title might not continue to fit as he grew older." Mary would find out soon enough that Leon would need a firm hand to control his orneriness, and she was determined to provide that.

"I refuse to raise our children without discipline," Mary told Kelly. "They will learn to have manners and behave themselves."

It was April and the weather was almost perfect. It was pleasantly cool in the mornings, and there was a chill to the evening air. Kelly still built a small fire in the potbellied stove that warmed their bedroom at night. This was mostly for Leon's comfort, not for theirs.

The week of the 12th, it rained every day. The seeds were in the ground and the sprouts began to break the surface. "This rain is just what we needed," Kelly said as he and Mary sat in front of the fireplace in the kitchen house. The small blaze was sufficient to ward off the damp that seeped in from outside. It was really comforting to Mary, sitting there, watching the flames dance and feeling their warmth. Listening to the patter of rain on the roof and the hiss of the drops as they dripped down the open chimney into the fire added to her contentment. She thought, *How utterly happy I am, with my husband beside me and my son cooing on my lap. We are rich in the things that matter. We've plenty to eat, a roof over our heads, and a clean bed to sleep in when we lay down at night.*

"Here, Kelly, take Leon." She sat him on his daddy's lap. "I'll put our supper on the table. It's almost Leon's bedtime, and I would like to sit and read a while before I fall asleep."

* * * * *

On the 18th of April, Mary awoke at the usual time. Kelly was already up and had gone to the kitchen house to make his pot of coffee. He had taken to doing that since Leon was born. That gave Mary a little extra time to sleep in the mornings, and she appreciated it. But this morning was different. As soon as Mary's feet touched the floor, a wave of nausea hit her. She grabbed the chamber pot from beneath their bed and threw up.

Oh my God, surely I can't be pregnant again, was the first thought she had. *Leon is only six months old.* She knew her monthly was late, but she hadn't considered the possibility of another baby. *Maybe something I had for supper last night just didn't sit well with my stomach. I won't say anything to Kelly just yet,* she thought. *He has enough on his mind.*

Within a week's time, Mary was almost certain. As soon as she sat upright in the mornings, the nausea swept over her. Kelly was already up each morning and out the door, so he had no idea she was experiencing morning sickness. Kelly was a smart man and noticed everything around him. He also recognized changes in people's demeanor, their routines, and their appearance. It was not easy for Mary to keep Kelly in the dark about any changes she was going through.

This was one secret she had to keep until just the right time. *I'll be on guard, not change any of my usual actions, and watch my facial expressions. I can't let my feelings show on my face, or Kelly will pick up immediately that something is different. I must know for sure before breaking the news to him.* This was one secret she had to keep until just the right time.

* * * * *

63

"Kelly, I haven't visited Peggy since we were there at Christmas time," Mary said in early May while they sat at the table having breakfast. "Do you think it would be ok for Leon and me to take the 'Swamp Rabbit' from Rayflin one morning next week and spend a day or two with Peggy and Tom?"

Kelly had a fleeting look of concern on his face, Mary noticed, before he answered. "Of course." He didn't mind the visit; it was just that it was the first time since their marriage that Mary had made such a suggestion. She and her sister kept in touch through regular letters to each other. Why all of a sudden did she want to take Leon on the train to visit? To Kelly, something was amiss with Mary's suggestion, but he had no way of knowing without actually asking her directly, and he didn't know how to approach her. *Well, who can explain the motivation of a woman?* he thought.

"I think that's a fine idea, Mary. Write to Peggy and tell her when to expect you two. I'll take y'all down to Rayflin and put you on the train whenever you say. It will be good for you to visit your sister; the weather has been so nice, and I know y'all have some catching up to do. Letters are just not the same as being there."

* * * * *

On the 25th of May, Mary and Leon arrived at the Batesburg depot. Peggy came with Tom this time to pick them up. They hugged excitedly and Tom and Peggy made a big to-do over how much Leon had grown.

"We're so glad you're here, Mary. We have so much to talk about." Peggy noticed a brief look of dismay.

"You know how lonesome it can be in the country," Mary replied.

As soon as Peggy and Mary were alone in the guest room, Peggy said, "Ok, fess up, Mary. I could tell as soon as you stepped from that train that something is troubling you, and I want to know what it is."

"I'm going to have another baby, Peggy," she blurted out. "I just don't know how to tell Kelly. Things are pretty hectic now with the crops and Kelly working at the store in the evenings. Leon is only six months old, and now we're going to have another child. I don't think I can handle two this close together, and money is tight. How am I going to tell him? And the house is so small…where will we put another baby?"

"Whoa! Just slow down, one worry at a time please. I tell you what you're going to do. You're going to sit him down and tell him. I don't know Kelly Gantt like you do, but I'll bet he will be thrilled at the news. He and his brothers are good at carpentry; they can add on to that house of yours. Babies are so precious, how could any man not be pleased? Maybe you'll have a little girl this time. Oh, I envy you so, Mary. For heaven's sake don't look so gloomy. Count your blessings."

"You're right, Peggy, I'm so glad I came. You always could make me feel better. Kelly is a good man and he is a proud father. I'll tell him as soon as I get back home."

"Well, I'm glad you came too. All you needed was someone to remind you that you have nothing to worry about."

The next day, Peggy went with Mary to the doctor's office, leaving Leon with Peggy's next door neighbor. Peggy vouched for Miss Martha as a wonderful and trustworthy person.

Dr. Timmerman examined Mary in his office. It was not a pleasant experience, but Peggy stayed at her side. "You are indeed with child, Mrs. Gantt," Dr. Timmerman confirmed. "I would estimate the child's due date around mid-December. Congratulations to you and Kelly. Have you told him the good news yet?"

"No, actually I haven't," Mary replied. "I wanted to be absolutely certain before I broke the news. Kelly has so much on his mind, I didn't want to add to his burdens."

"Don't worry," Dr. Timmerman said. "I'm sure he will be pleased. Pretty soon, it will be obvious. I suggest you tell him and quit worrying about it."

Now all Mary had to do was break the news to Kelly. She thought, *Just tell him, huh. If only it were that easy.*

* * * * *

When Mary and the Leon arrived at Rayflin on the train two days later, Kelly was there to pick them up.

"I have surely been lonesome without my little family," he told Mary when they stepped down from the train.

Every evening, Kelly helped run the store until closing time. Business was going pretty well. They had regular customers now. The local boys often stopped for visiting and a drink. But while there, they always purchased a few things.

When Mary arrived, Kelly suggested, "Why don't you visit our store before we head home? You haven't been inside since we opened."

Mary agreed, smiling up at her husband and nodding her head

in the affirmative. Kelly took her arm and helped guide her over the uneven ground between the passenger shed and the store entrance. Mary was holding Leon. Once inside, she passed him to Kelly so she could take in the organization and arrangement of the store building.

When they entered, Roston was behind the counter assisting a customer. Mary was pleasantly surprised at what she saw. Every item was clearly priced. The shelves were neat and clean and the counters on either side of the room thoroughly shined from polishing. There was a wood stove in the center for heating, several chairs for customers to sit a spell, a table with a checker board, a pickle barrel, and glass jars of sweets to entice the young'uns. All created a comfortable atmosphere, with the objective of customers lingering and purchasing more than the one thing they had come to get.

"Why, Kelly, you and Roston have done a wonderful job. Everything is so neatly organized, and you seem to have a good stock of the necessities, pantry staples, and tools, bolts of cloth, buttons and such to interest the ladies. I am very impressed."

"You have Kelly to thank for the organization, Mary. Me, I mostly enjoy visiting with the folks. This is about the most enjoyable job I've had. It sure beats working in the fields with Pa, and the queer part is, we're actually clearing a little profit," Roston replied.

* * * * *

Later that evening, Mary and Kelly sat in their kitchen house. She stood facing Kelly with her back to the fireplace. Little Leon had already been put in his cradle for the night.

"Kelly, I have something to tell you," Mary declared, twisting a strand of her hair around her finger, a signal of nervous anticipation.

"I've always been good at reading people and I thought a little something wasn't sitting right with you the last few weeks."

"Well, to put it plain and simple, I'm going to have another baby."

Kelly took Mary's hand and pulled her down onto his lap. "And why would that trouble you? I think that is wonderful news," he said as he kissed her cheek.

"Oh Kelly, do you really mean that? I was so afraid you would be upset. I know you are so busy with the farm and the store. And we don't have much money. Where are we going to put another child?"

"You let me worry about that, Mary. I've been thinking for a while now that we need to add on to the house. You know my brothers will help with the building and Pa has plenty of good pine on the place. We could have Job Hall and his boys cut the timber and saw the lumber at that sawmill of theirs across the river. We may have to wait a few months though. I promised to help Roston build his house next to the store. He already has the lumber ready. Roston bought the old Smith Branch School building over towards the chalk mine. He had some boys tear it down for the lumber. Just as soon as his house is finished, Roston will be more than happy to help add on to ours. I'll start drawing on the plans right away. Everything will be fine, you'll see."

Mary turned and planned a big kiss on Kelly's lips. "Kelly, you are good to me and I feel so much better now that you know."

"Another baby, I am more than pleased! Excited is a better description. Could we have a girl this time, Mary?"

"I'll do my best, but you know, Kelly, there are no guarantees."

"Leon will have a playmate and will be a big brother. Do you have any idea when we can expect this blessed addition?"

"Doc Timmerman calculates around mid-December."

"Aw! That was it, I was wondering about your sudden need to take the train and visit your sister. This baby will be an early Christmas present; I can't think of anything I'd rather have more."

Seven

FROM HIS PRECARIOUS PERCH ON THE ROOF OF ROSTON'S house, Kelly could see up the road to the Northeast. To his left about three hundred yards away he could see his pa's cotton fields stretching to the horizon. Kel and his workers were in the fields, chopping the weeds from around the young cotton plants. The workers, the Burketts and the Hardys, were black families who sharecropped on the place along with a single black fellow by the name of Arthur Moore. They helped Kel with the crops in exchange for a share of the profits, a place to live, and a little garden spot of their own.

To Kelly's right, and only one hundred feet from his perch on the roof, stood Kel and Peninnah's house. Here, the road began an S loop down towards the river. As the road turned slightly to the north, Kel's house sat near the edge, at the middle curve of the S, then the road turned south, crossed the railroad tracks, passed in front of the store and Roston's new house, then looped back to the north before crossing the North Edisto River. Behind him, Kelly could see the black water of the river, less than one hundred fifty yards away, meandering south.

* * * * *

It was already mid-June and the temperature at noon was unbearably hot. The tin roof soaked up heat and reflected it back in his face. He and Roston had started nailing the tin on early this morning but would have to quit pretty soon. With the sun beating down on it, the tin felt almost too hot to handle, even wearing gloves.

When the sun gets low in the west this afternoon, Kelly thought, *we'll be able to finish the roofing.*

"It sure is getting hot up here, Kelly," Roston stated as he took a break from hammering and looked up. The ends of his dark hair were wet and plastered against his cheek; beads of sweat glistened on his forehead as he removed his wide-brimmed straw hat, wiping his forehead with his shirt sleeve. "I think it's about time for us to knock off until this evening. We should be able to finish up then."

Roston's house was almost finished. As soon as the roof and some work on the inside was completed, he would be able to move in. The house stood only forty feet from the store, with enough room between the two to pass through to the wagon sheds down near the river. With Sam, Woodard and Kelly helping, the building was almost complete in less than two months. Being so near to the store, Roston could work on his house and keep an eye out for customers at the same time. The brothers were up in the cotton fields with their pa and the workers.

"As soon as I get moved in, Kelly, we'll get to work on your place."

Climbing down the ladder propped against the back of the roof, they retreated across the road to their parents' back porch and the shade of the large magnolia standing there. Roston worked the pitcher pump furiously, filling a bucket with cool water. They poured water in the wash pan, took turns scrubbing away the sweat and grime with a bar of octagon soap, poured dippers full of water over their heads, and drank long gulps from the bucket. They sat in the shade under the magnolia to cool off and continue their conversation concerning their building plans.

"We best better wait until the weather turns cold again to cut the pines for the building," intoned Kelly. "Pa says there's a good stand of pines on the place about a quarter of a mile up the railroad towards Steadman, but it's too dangerous to be cutting trees in the summertime. They're some awfully big rattlesnakes in these woods, as you well know. We'll just wait until after first frost. I've about got the plans drawn up, and if the house is ready by next spring, we'll be satisfied. The new baby will be sleeping in the cradle for a while and we already have that other room for Leon."

Three weeks later, on July 11th, the house was completed enough for Roston to move in. Of course, the moving part didn't take long, since he only had his bed and clothes to move from his pa and ma's across the road.

"It sure is a nice feeling to have your own place," Roston said as he and Kelly set the bed up in the front room. "Single men don't need much, just a table and a couple of chairs. Ma said I could have my meals with them. I won't need a stove. Maybe a few dishes, glasses mostly. If company drops by, we'll have to have a drink, of course. I believe we did a right good job. Thanks, Kelly."

True to his word, as soon as Roston's house was completed, Kelly started serious consideration on the addition to theirs. Mary and Kelly discussed the building plans almost every night around the supper table in the kitchen house.

* * * * *

"We'll be ready to cut the timber and have the lumber sawed as soon as the weather gets cold," said Kelly. "I've got the plans all drawn out, Mary. Take a look and see if they meet with your approval." He got up from the table to retrieve his rolled-up drawing from the mantelpiece.

He spread the paper out on the kitchen table and secured the corners with a jelly jar, their empty tea glasses, and the butter dish. Using his index finger as a pointer, he said, "We're adding four rooms, two on either side, with a large center hallway. The rooms will be about fourteen by fourteen feet and the hall about six feet across."

"They will be such nice big rooms. I can't imagine so much more space." Mary beamed up at him as he continued his explanation.

"I thought we would attach the new part at the end of our bedroom. That would mean four rooms in a line across the back of the house, then the hallway and another two rooms to the front. It's sort of an upside-down L shape, with the long part being the back and the front addition the shorter part. We'll have a porch all the way across the front and a door to the outside on both ends of the hallway. I thought we would add a porch on this other end too. With doors on both ends of the hall, we should be able to catch the breeze through the house."

"That will help during the humid summer months. In the evenings after nightfall, I do love to sit on the porch, listening to the crickets and whippoorwills and watching the lightening bugs in the woods across the road. Doors open on both ends of the hall would help circulate the air if there is any breeze blowing, and we will have screen doors on both ends; we won't need to close the interior wooden doors. How expensive will the addition be? More importantly, can we afford it?" Mary asked, biting her bottom lip, a sure sign of exasperation.

"Sure, Mary. Pa's giving us the pines for the lumber. I can get some of the fellows around here to help with the cutting, and Job Hall won't charge much to saw the trees into lumber. I'll go to Smith's lumber yard in Batesburg and have them make the windows for the new house. All total, it shouldn't cost more than about fifteen-hundred. Roston, Sam, and Woodard have already offered to help me build. Rion and Buck want to help too. We'll get it done, you'll see."

"Oh, Kelly, that sounds wonderful. I'm so excited about your plans."

All the Gantt brothers were good at carpentry, a definite inherited talent from that side of the family. If one of them needed a house built, they were all willing to pitch in and help. Some were also good at making furniture, like Kelly.

There was always camaraderie between the brothers. Roston, Woodard, Cyrus and Rion were easier going, not as likely to stir up trouble if it could be avoided; the other three, Kelly, Sam, and Buck, were more likely to go looking for trouble and generally found it. But when a dirty deed was directed at one brother, they were all willing to take up for the offended. That's how they all were; it was a bond between brothers.

That's how they approached the building of Kelly and Mary's new house. The brothers all volunteered, and didn't have to be asked.

* * * * *

By August, it was steamy hot in the middle of the day—dog days, the old folks called it. There seemed to be not a breath of air stirring anywhere, the yellow flies bit unmercifully, and gnats hovered around your eyes and nose, just waiting to retrieve any drop of moisture. Sand gnats especially tormented Leon. Whenever Mary took him outside and sat him down in the shade while she worked, they attacked his little eyes and nose and set him crying from their assaults. She was constantly wiping his eyes and batting the little insects away. But Mary couldn't keep Leon in the house when she had outside chores. He had to be under her watchful eye, lest he get into trouble. Leon had started to pull himself up and had even taken a step or two holding on to the kitchen chairs. But usually when Mary had to go outside, he was content to just sit in the shade, watching her, playing with the wooden spoons she had given him, and babbling to himself.

Mary's morning sickness had long since passed. She was doing fine, except for the burden of carrying two babies, one on her hip and the other in her belly. One Monday in late August, Mary headed down to the spring for water.

"It's still early, just good daylight," Mary said to Leon, who was perched on her hip. "In August, it pays to do outside work early in the day or late in the evening. You'll learn that soon enough, Son."

It's a little cooler this morning, she thought as she carried Leon and a bucket of water from the spring up the slight incline towards their backyard. There was a wide wooden bench holding three large steel washtubs. She began filling the first tub with the water and then started back to the spring for another.

Leon couldn't be left alone in the backyard, not even for the five-minute trek to and from the spring. He could get himself into too much trouble in five minutes…or trouble could find him.

Mary envisioned, with a smile, the mess Leon had gotten into a month earlier. There were no screens in the windows. As a consequence, Mary's Dominique hens invaded the house, flying in through the windows. It was almost impossible to keep them out with the heat; the windows had to be up. Leon was ecstatic, crawling around on the floor with the chickens. When she realized what he had found, he was in a smelly mess. He had smeared chicken poop on his face and hands. Jerking him up from the floor to clean his face, she asked Kelly, "Do you think this child can't smell or taste?" It was comical now, but at the time, she was thoroughly disgusted.

So Mary, struggling with the bucket and Leon, made at least eight or ten trips to get the tubs full of water to wash their clothes and filled the black iron pot in the center of the yard. She had already prepared the wood for a fire under it and as soon as she had it filled, she would light the fire to heat the water. This was her washday, and she knew it would take her most of the day to finish her task. After the tubs were filled, she made one more trip for water. This she poured into a smaller foot tub and set it out in the sun to heat up. Leon would need a good bath after playing in the sand under that big chinaberry tree all day.

When the water finally started to boil, she put Kelly's dirty overalls in and every so often stirred them around with a long tree branch. After they had boiled well, she ladled them out and put them in the first washtub on the bench. Here she used a scrub board and lye soap to clean them thoroughly. Then they were wrung out, placed in the second tub to rinse, squeezed out again, and put into the last tub to get out any left-over soap. After the final rinse, she wrung them out once more and hung them on her clothesline to dry. *In this heat, they should all be dried before sundown,* she thought. She repeated the same process with all their dirty garments until all had been cleaned, then she tipped the tubs up and let the water pour onto the ground.

The water splashing on the ground was more than Leon could resist. Mary turned her back just long enough to check the clothes on the line. By the time she turned around, Leon had crawled over to the puddle and was laughing and splashing in the dirty water. Mary couldn't help but smile at her son's antics.

"You are really going to need that bath now, young man." She giggled. Mary sat down on the back steps and just let him splash and play for a while. "It won't hurt a thing for you to have a little fun, and I don't mind sitting down for a spell," said Mary. *It surely is hot, even here in the shade.* With her cotton blouse sticking to her skin and her feet sweating in her high-topped shoes, Mary was miserable. *I'll just take these off for a few minutes,* she thought as she pulled her long skirt up to her knees and unlaced the shoes. *It feels so good to wiggle my toes; I'll remove my hose as well. Sister Peggy would be absolutely scandalized to see me sitting here like this—no shoes or hose and my skirt pulled up.* She sat for a while, the feel of the warm breeze brushing her cheek, her feet absorbing the heat of the wooden steps, and the sounds of Leon splashing and laughing in the dirty puddle echoing across the yard. Finally deciding she had wasted enough time relaxing, Mary put her hose and shoes back on, stood, placed her hands on her hips and arched her back. "Time to get that bath, Son."

* * * * *

When Kelly came back to the house from the fields, Mary had just finished giving Leon his much-needed bath and was in the kitchen house preparing their supper. "I went ahead and milked the cow for you," he said as he extended the milk bucket.

"Thank you, Kelly. Just pour it in that crock on the table please and take it down to the spring. That's the only way to keep it from spoiling in this heat."

"Do you want to fix a bottle for Leon before I take it?"

"That's a good idea."

Leon had been weaned from her breast and now he was taking a bottle filled with milk from their cow; he was seemingly doing fine.

"I think, Mary, I'm going to build you an ice chest. I made the one Roston has in his store for drinks and it works pretty well. We can at least keep Leon's milk from spoiling for a while and we can have ice blocks brought in on the train every week. Roston does for the store. We'll just tell him to order ice for us too."

"It would be wonderful, not to have to make the trip down to the spring to fix Leon's bottles," said Mary. "It seems like I spend a good part of my day going back and forth to the spring to fetch perishables. How are the crops coming along, Kelly?"

"Just fine; we had enough rain early in the season and the cotton bolls are all opening. If the weather holds, I think we'll have a good harvest. The corn is filled out too. Tomorrow, I'll pull you some roasting ears from the corn and we can have fresh corn for our supper."

Eight

THE HEAT OF AUGUST FINALLY GAVE WAY TO COOL BREEZES and falling leaves. By late October, Kelly and the boys were able to get in the woods to cut the pines without fear of snakes. The stand of pines Kel had told his son about would be more than enough lumber to build the addition on their house.

"My, Pa was sure right about this stand of pines," Kelly remarked to the others. "They're at least twenty-four inches in diameter and fifty-five feet tall. They can be seen for miles, standing like sentinels in the North Edisto river swamp, and they're beautiful to behold. And the best part, they're not so far from the railroad bed; we shouldn't have such a rough time getting to 'em."

Most of the leaves had already fallen from the hardwoods that mingled with the tall pines near the river. Tom Hardy and Arthur Moore helped Kelly, Sam, and Woodard cut the pines with crosscut saws.

When the trees were felled, they were limbed up, chains wrapped around their trunks, and dragged to Rayflin by mules. Job Hall's sawmill was across the river not too far from Rayflin, and he and his boys began transporting the pine logs there to be cut into lumber.

As soon as the lumber had been cut to Kelly's satisfaction, it was hauled back to Rayflin in wagons and stored in one of Kel's sheds, out of the weather. The lumber would remain there, stacked with spacers between the boards to dry. After a couple months under the sheds, the lumber would be ready to dress, plane to a smooth finish in preparation for building.

The lumber had been stacked in Kel's sheds down at Rayflin for a good six weeks when the winter storm hit.

The trip back and forth to the kitchen house became too much for Mary to endure with freezing temperatures and a light snow on the ground. Leon was walking now and had to be constantly watched by his mother. She couldn't leave him unattended in the main house for fear he would burn himself on the wood stove. When she went to the kitchen house, he had to toddle along in her footsteps. Mary was more than eight months along in her pregnancy and unable to carry him.

"With this snow covering the road down to Rayflin," Kelly spoke aloud to Mary, "and without a sled, it's impossible to travel any distance."

"Well, Kelly," Mary said, "at least we have plenty of wood to keep the fires burning in the fireplace and the cook stove. You, Leon, and I will have to huddle together here in the kitchen house. We could sleep on pallets on the floor in front of the fire if necessary, and I can cook our food. The salt box still has a few rabbits in it and you could make it to the smoke house if need be. There's also plenty of kerosene and matches and the water barrel is outside. You could chip up some of the ice on top and I could melt it on the stove or even get a bowl full of snow. We really are fortunate, much better off than some of our neighbors, I'm sure."

"I don't see how you can sleep on a pallet in your condition,

Mary. That baby is due in a couple of weeks. How in God's name do you think you can lie on the floor! I can see the logic of sleeping here, but you can't sleep on this floor. I'll get water hot on the stove, melt the ice on the steps to the main house, and bring Leon's cot out here. Make a list of what else you need from the main house; I'll get it before the snow gets any deeper. I think I can rig up some snow shoes. I'll have to be getting in wood, going back and forth to the barn to feed our animals and to milk the cow. We'll be fine; staying out here is the most sensible thing to do."

Beginning December fifth, the snow started falling in earnest; it snowed off and on for three days. Kelly was right. Mary fared much better on the cot than on the floor. They huddled in front of the fire, wind howled around the kitchen house, the window shutters rattled, and the world outside became a winter wonderland. Along with the howling wind, they heard snaps and pops from outside in the storm.

"What is all that noise, Kelly? It's louder than the wind whipping around outside. I even thought I heard howling in the direction of the swamp. It was a freighting cry; gave me goose bumps knowing some wild creature is so near."

"I'm sure the snapping is limbs breaking and crashing to the ground. As far as the howling, it could be a wolf. Pa claims he has heard them in swamp recently. I thought they were gone in this part of the country. Maybe they're not. Don't be afraid, we're safe with the window shutters and door closed, and I have my shotgun propped in the corner."

At night, the cot was pulled up close to the fire. It was still cold on the far side of the room; the windows and door were far from airtight. Leon slept on the cot with his mother. Her body heat kept him snug and a chair pushed up to the cot kept him from falling off.

On his homemade snow shoes, Kelly took care of everything except the cooking. The storm finally cleared on the evening of the third day, leaving twelve inches of snow behind and limbs covering the yard. The wind and heavy snow had snapped them and icicles hung twelve inches from the roofs of every building. This was unusual for South Carolina, and few of the old folks could remember ever seeing a storm of this magnitude in their community.

"I only wish I knew how the folks at Rayflin are faring. But Pa has all the brothers to help and I know they are well stocked with all the necessities. I'll get down there as soon as the weather warms up and I can travel." Kelly was trying to be positive. Mary still noticed concern evident in his voice as he opened a window shutter to look out. Broken limbs were scattered all over the yard. Kelly thought to himself, *The road to Rayflin might be impassable, blocked by fallen trees maybe.* "What does Leon think of all this snow?" Kelly asked, trying to change the subject.

"Every time you open the door, he looks in wonderment at the beauty outside and wants to get out in it. I have to hold him back or he would be outside with you, which is quite normal for a child," replied Mary. "When I was a child, I felt the same way, didn't you?"

"If I'm able to get everything situated that we need, maybe I'll just bundle him up and take him outside. We could get a big bowl full of clean snow and make some snow cream like my Ma used to do for us. Do you know how to make it, Mary?"

"Of course I do, silly. I haven't done that since I was a child, but it's easy and something he would probably love."

"The morning we walked out here to the kitchen house when the snow first started falling, Leon had some trouble toddling behind me," Mary remembered, a smile touching her lips. "He followed behind me in the path, but the snow was falling and already collecting on every surface. It wasn't yet so deep, but he fell twice before we got inside. He didn't cry though; he thought it was funny. If I didn't have a time trying to get him up those steps in my condition…I can just imagine what we must have looked like. I couldn't help but laugh too after we finally got inside."

"The snow storm was over in three days, but it lingered on the ground far longer. For now, we'll just have to wait it out until the temperature warms up and all this snow melts."

"Well, I for one will be glad to see it gone. It's hard enough for me to get around with Leon at my heels and this baby on the way. This snow creates such a hardship for people living in the country, with no way to travel and our livestock to feed, not to mention trying to stay warm. I'm ready for some sunshine."

The snow finally departed, melting away in the bright sunshine of the clear, cold days that followed. The temperature rose into the high 30s, warm enough to get rid of the snow but cold nevertheless.

Nine

LESS THAN TWO WEEKS AFTER THE BIG SNOW STORM, ON THE 18th of December, Mary's baby arrived. Kelly was home that morning and went to fetch Miss Hannah as soon as Mary was sure it was labor. Leon had to go along with his daddy; Mary was in no condition to watch him.

Leon sat next to Kelly on the buggy seat, bundled up for warmth inside one of Mary's thick quilts and so excited about a trip with his daddy he forgot about causing trouble. He sat still as a statue on the thick leather seat, watching the trees pass by on the side of the narrow, two rut road, amazed at all the noise coming from the woods; the trees in the woods were bare of foliage, except for the evergreens. A covey of quail flew up from the woodland floor. and several rabbits and squirrels scampered across in front of the buggy as they passed.

Shortly, the woods thinned and an old wood clapboard house with a porch on the front appeared a short distance from the main road to their right. Kelly pulled the right rein, saying aloud, "Gee!" which, in the language of plowing mules, meant right. "Haw," he said and a tugged on the left rein. The mule turned in beside the house. *Surprising what a mule can learn,* Kelly thought. *They're a heap smarter than some humans I know.*

"Whoa!" Kelly exclaimed while pulling back on the reins. The mule came to a stop; Kelly picked up Leon and his quilt and bounded up the steps to knock on the door. An old lady appeared and after a brief conversation with Kelly, said, "Give me just a couple of minutes to grab my bag and tell my husband Bill what's up and I'll be out.

You and Leon go ahead and get situated in the buggy; I can manage to climb in myself on the other side. Maybe the young mister will share that quilt of his to help keep these old bones warm on the way back to help his mother."

Leon was amazed at the old lady, Miss Hannah, who was now sitting beside him sharing his cover. He gazed up at the gray squiggles of hair escaping from beneath her blue bonnet, not uttering a sound; he stared in amazement at the ample woman smiling down at him. He didn't seem upset, too absorbed in watching her every move and listening to her questioning Kelly about his mother, Mary.

Soon, they arrived back at their home. Even Leon, at the tender age of fourteen months, showed shock when the old lady hopped out of the buggy by herself and hurried up the front steps as soon as the buggy came to a halt. She was entering his parents' bedroom while Kelly was lifting him out of the buggy and tying the reigns around the old piece of iron rail sticking up from the ground in front of their house. "I need to get you inside where it is warm, young man; I can see to the mule and buggy later."

As it happened, Roston stopped by for a visit and relieved Kelly for a little, keeping an eye on Leon while Kelly put the mule in the barn. He knew later he would have to hitch her back up to get Miss Hannah home, but there was no telling how long the birth would take, and he couldn't in good conscience leave the mule out in the cold.

The labor was long and painful for Mary, but this time she knew what to expect and was prepared. She consoled herself throughout the ordeal knowing the memory of it would fade as soon as that sweet little angel was placed in her arms. The baby finally arrived late in the evening at around 5:00 p.m., a real little dark-haired beauty, and the spitting image of her mother. They named her Louise—no middle name, just Louise Gantt.

Mother and baby were doing fine when Miss Hannah finally departed. Mary had been the sole caregiver for Leon before the baby came, but for the next couple of weeks, that chore would fall to Kelly. Kelly sent word by one of his hands to Rayflin with the news of Louise's birth. His pa and ma arrived early the next morning to see their new granddaughter, but the novelty of a new baby had dimmed somewhat to the grandparents. Their daughter Corrie had a baby girl, so Louise was their third, and they were expecting to have many more. Penninah stayed the night with them and offered to take Leon to Rayflin until Mary was back on her feet.

"I appreciate the offer, Ma, but I can take care of Leon myself," Kelly said.

He would live to regret refusing his momma's generous offer. The two weeks that followed Louise's birth, Kelly Gantt developed a new appreciation for motherhood. Every step he took, Leon was with him, either toddling along behind or carried in his daddy's arms. When Kelly went up to the barn to feed the mules and their old milk cow, Leon was with him. Leon especially seemed to enjoy watching Kelly milk the cow. The only problem was he wanted to help or stick his small hands into the bucket as the milk streamed in. Kelly finally solved this problem by pinning Leon between his thighs just out of reach of the bucket.

Whenever Kelly took a bucket of slop up to the pigpen, Leon, ever the little helper, picked up sticks and leaves, poked his little hands through the wire, and added these to the pig trough.

"Boy, what am I going to do with you? I'll sure be glad when your momma can take charge of you again. Tending to you and keeping you out of trouble is a full-time job."

Mary was soon back on her feet and Kelly was free to help Roston in the store and work on dressing his lumber under the shed at Rayflin. "Boy, it sure is nice to go back to work," he said to Roston as soon as he came in the door. "I can tell you from experience, tending to little children is no picnic." Relating his experiences to Roston with Leon, he added "Tending to that boy was like trying to catch a greased pig. Remember this advice: if Ma ever offers to tend to one of your young'uns, let her."

Ten

THE FLOOR AND CEILING JOISTS, AS WELL AS THE STUDS FOR the inside walls, could be left rough cut, with weather boarding only for the outside, tongue and groove for the inside walls, and ceilings planed to a smooth finish. By the end of February, all the lumber had been dressed and the building could begin.

March 6, 1912, Kelly, Sam, Roston and Woodard begin laying out the foundation for the new addition according to Kelly's plans. Planting season had not begun in earnest, and besides, their pa had farmhands on the place to help while his boys were busy at Kelly's. Rion had been left in charge of running Roston's store with the help of their youngest brother, Buck. Rion was fourteen years old, Buck was twelve, and they both thought being in charge at the store would be a whole lot more fun than helping with the building or the crops.

"I just hope those two nitwits don't find that jug I have hidden under the counter at the store!" exclaimed Roston, worry in his voice. "If they find it, they'll surely drink it and Ma will have my hide. I better remember to take it over to my house just so they won't be tempted."

"That probably would be a good idea, Roston," Kelly agreed.

"Remove the temptation while you can. Ma and Pa would sure give you hell if Rion and Buck turned up drunk."

When they had the dimensions of the house laid out, Kelly and the brothers set the foundation blocks to support the floor. These were huge blocks of heart pine, buried about twelve inches in the ground and placed at intervals of twelve feet along the outside dimensions and where all weight-bearing walls would stand. After the blocks were in place. they had to be leveled to exact measurements. After this task was completed, they could begin with the floor joists and the framing.

For two weeks, the weather cooperated and the brothers worked from daylight to dark. Mary had their breakfast ready when they arrived at 6:00 a.m., fixed their dinner at 12:00 noon, and in between carried them glasses of tea and water. Minding Louise and Leon, cooking for the men-folk, and tending to their livestock kept Mary busy. She had not a minute to herself and fell into bed exhausted every night. Of course, she wasn't the only one; Kelly had been working just as hard. After the first two weeks, work on the house was sporadic, as spring rains caused delays.

"The house is really beginning to take shape, Mary," Kelly said at supper in mid-May. "Without my brothers helping me, it would be a really big job. It would take so much longer. As it is, if the weather stays pretty, we'll have the roof on in a week, then I can work on the inside by myself. I know Roston needs to get back to running the store before our little brothers cause a major disaster. They have really done pretty well except for extending credit to a few people that don't pay their bills. They're just a couple of young boys and don't want to say no when someone asks for credit."

On June twenty-fifth, the new addition was complete and Kelly and Mary moved in. The original two rooms became their dining room and kitchen. The new addition included the front parlor, three bedrooms, and the wide hallway between. The only problem to Mary was the absence of a connecting passageway between the old and new parts of the house. To get to the bedrooms, one had to exit through the dining room or kitchen onto the front porch and cross to the hallway entrance. This wasn't a major problem and Mary didn't complain. It was so much better than braving the elements to get to the kitchen house; at least the front porch was covered. The new part of the house really looked nice and the increase in space was dramatic. A stark difference in the two sections was quite evident. The new lumber was the color of freshly churned butter; the old section was drab, dark gray with slashes of bright orange where fat lighter of the pine lumber was exposed.

That first night, they all slept contently in their new surroundings. Leon had his own room; Louise was still in the cradle in Kelly and Mary's room. Once during the night, Mary left her bed to check on her children. The first thing she noticed was the smell of the fresh pine lumber. There was full moon and Mary needed no lamp to light her way as she tiptoed in to check on Leon. The moonlight streamed through the open window and fell across his bed. His tousled head lay on the pillow and Mary could hear the rhythm of his breathing. "My, but you are a little angel when you are asleep, Son," she whispered. Bending over, she kissed his moist cheek before returning to her bed, so content with her family and her new house.

As the days passed, they had quite a few visitors. Neighbors just had to stop when passing by, giving their opinions freely as to the building and how it could have been improved. Mostly they were just curious and saw an opportunity to stop by and talk a spell.

Most of the community was all a buzz about the big stump meeting to take place in Steadman on the fourth of July.

Alice and Henderson Hall, who lived south of Rayflin in the Sugar Bottom community, stopped by on the twenty-seventh of June to see the new addition and visit.

"Y'all going to the stump meeting at Steadman, Kelly?" Henderson asked. Not waiting for Kelly's reply, Henderson began droning on about the big celebration and local politics. "I hear Abe Hall and his boys will be barbequing eight or ten pigs for the celebration. The election in November is going to be a close one, you know, at least for the sheriff's office. Thaddeus Corley and that fellow Willie Shumpert from over near Lexington are in a tight race I understand. They're both good speakers I hear." He added emphatically, "There ain't a nickel's worth of difference between um! The big question of course, state wise, is the dispensary system. In my opinion, it's about time they did away with the state meddling in the liquor business."

Silently Kelly was thinking, *Henderson is just full of opinions today*, but he said nothing, just continued his struggle to appear interested in Henderson's opinions.

"Of course, the sheriff ain't got anything to say about state politics, but I understand the fellows running for district legislators will be there." Dropping his voice to a conspiratorial tone, he continued, "I hear Governor Colie L. Blease himself will be in attendance. He won't have any competition in November because he's running unopposed again. No black-hearted Republican even filed to run; knew it would be a losing battle I guess. The politicians will be footing the bill for the pigs and all the ladies will be bringing the fixings and they'll be plenty of lemonade and probably some stronger refreshment. Y'all are going to be there I hope."

Finally, Henderson paused for Kelly's reply. "Well, Henderson, to be honest, I haven't thought a whole lot about it. Abe Hall has asked me and my brothers to build the speakers stand for the celebration, but I haven't committed to doing it yet. I guess I will though, could be a mite interesting and I don't mind helping out. What do you think, Mary?"

"I think it would be good, Kelly, to get away for a few hours, and I would like to visit with our neighbors. Let's go."

Eleven

SATURDAY, JULY FOURTH, BEGAN THE SAME AS EVERY OTHER steamy, summer day in South Carolina. The mercury had reached 95 degrees two weeks before and had hovered there, unwavering, except when the evening sun dropped below the horizon to the west. Then and only then did the unbearable heat of midday lift a bit, allowing a breath of coolness to cover the land. Even a dip in temperature of ten degrees was welcome respite from the stifling heat of midday.

I'll have to do my cooking for the July fourth celebration late the evening before, Mary concluded to herself. *I would pass out from the heat standing in front of that wood cook stove during mid-day.* She made three apple pies using dried apples she preserved, two gallons of sweet tea, and a huge pot of white rice.

All her food, when cooled sufficiently, was stored in the cooling chest Kelly made. It had become a necessity in her kitchen to keep their food and Leon's milk from spoiling. Kelly made the chest 3x5 feet in juniper wood, along with the hinged lid covered it in tin, and built another juniper box to set down inside the tin covered chest. That box was two inches smaller than the first on all sides; sawdust was packed tightly between the inside box and the outside one.

Blocks of ice were delivered on the train along with Roston's order and were put inside to keep the contents cool. Whenever Roston ordered blocks of ice for the store drink box, he ordered ice for Mary too. *Thank heavens I have a cooling chest or all this food would have to be sealed up and sit down in the spring or it would ruin in this heat.*

Mounds of rice smothered with barbeque hash would be part of the main course at the picnic on the fourth, along with pounds of chopped pork thoroughly mixed with tangy barbeque sauce. Every family attending would bring a picnic basket filled with side dishes and drinks to compliment the main course of meat and hash.

It was nearing 9:00 in the morning on the fourth and time for the family to head up to Steadman. The road in front of their house had been busy since 7:00 a.m. with wagons, automobiles, and all manner of conveyances carrying folks to the celebration. Every time a vehicle passed by, dust swirled from its passing and left a cloud hanging in the air. The weeds that choked the ditches beside the road were coated with dust and the grimy smell had filled the air all morning.

Kelly was in no big hurry to get there. He had worked with the men-folk at Steadman for the last four days preparing for the big event.

A platform was constructed to accommodate the speakers and a long pit dug to hold the hot hickory coals for the barbequing. Tables and chairs were commandeered from every household in the community and set up under the big open shed at the head of Abe Hall's pond. Kelly and his brothers had worked on the construction of the speakers' platform and the ladies in Steadman had draped the front with red, white, and blue bunting.

Mr. Abe was in charge of preparing and cooking the eight pigs, each weighing a good one hundred pounds, over the hickory coals. He had a large contingency of local fellows who had volunteered to help with the barbequing. They had butchered and cleaned the pigs and put them on iron spits, where they would turn regularly over the pit late in the evening of the third and be slow cooked all night. It was a big barbequing party for the men-folk; not only did they barbeque the pigs, they also more or less barbequed themselves with moonshine furnished by some of the local distributors.

It was Abe Hall's job to keep a tight rein on his assistants so that neither the meat nor the helpers would be overdone when time for the big celebration arrived. Some of his helpers thought it was proper to drink 'a fifth on the third to celebrate the fourth' and Mr. Abe had to strictly monitor these boys so they wouldn't overdo it.

Abe had told Kelly the evening before, "Man, I won't be so foolish as to volunteer to be in charge of this kind of affair again. Cooking the meat is one thing, but trying to get this bunch of young yahoos to behave is another. I am much obliged to you, Kelly, and your brothers for helping me keep them in line. It's ok to have a friendly drink around the pit but half of these fellows would end up in it if y'all and a couple of others hadn't been here to help."

By the time Kelly had arrived home in the wee hours of the morning on the fourth, everything was under control and going well. Of course, Sam and Roston had been obliged to escort a couple of the troublemakers home, but they had left without a fight, only to return later in a somewhat more sober state when the festivities began in earnest.

Mary had their picnic baskets packed and the children scrubbed and cleaned by nine-thirty.

"I guess we better be going if we want a spot in the shade," Kelly said. Leon was all excited about riding in the buggy with his parents and could sense something unusual in the air. He sat on the seat between them while baby Louise sat on her mother's lap. It was only two miles from their house to Steadman. The last half-mile was a long, straight stretch, and before they reached the train depot on the outskirts, they could hear the noise of the crowd and the sound of a banjo and smell hickory and barbeque pork wafting through the air.

"My, there is a good crowd of people here today," said Mary.

There were buggies, wagons, and a few automobiles parked under every shady tree. Kelly found a spot for them not a hundred feet from the picnic shed and platform. Abe's youngest boy, John, was standing under the large red oak and waved to them to pull in. "Pa sent me over here with strict instructions to save this spot for Mr. Kelly," John said. "You are entitled, Pa says, for all your help."

"Why thank you, John, we certainly do appreciate Abe's consideration."

Kelly got down from the buggy, tied the mule to a low limb, and took baby Louise just long enough for Mary to climb down. By the time their feet had touched the ground, Kel and Peninnah appeared. Kel picked Leon up from the buggy and Kelly retrieved their picnic baskets from behind the seat. They all headed over to the shed, where ladies were placing food on the table. Kelly took Louise from her mother and he and his pa, with the children in tow, began to circulate among their neighbors. Every family in the community was represented. These people were all hard-working country folk and opportunities to relax and communicate with their neighbors were few and far between. The picnic baskets were emptied on the long row of serving tables and then most of ladies returned to their visiting. Dinner would be served at noon and it was still too early to uncover their food for fear of the ever-buzzing insects.

Mary and Peninnah strolled over to the shade of an enormous sycamore tree, where the rest of the Gantt family was sitting and talking with some of their neighbors. All of Kelly's brothers except for Cyrus, of course, were present, and so were sisters Jennie and Corrie, along with Corrie's husband, Jule Smith, and baby Nina Lee.

Several of the local musicians—brothers Amos and Jake Hallman, Tillman Reeves, and Cape Gunter—had set up on the platform and were entertaining the crowd with a little music. Amos Hallman was a first-rate banjo player, Jake and Tillman played fiddles, and Cape accompanied with his guitar. It wouldn't be a celebration without some lively music.

"I see some of our aspiring politicians are present," said Woodard. "I spoke to Thaddeus Corley and Willie Shumpert. Both seem to be good fellows, but I believe Corley will be reelected. I've heard it's better to stick with the devil you know rather than the devil you don't."

Roston, seated in a cane-bottomed chair leaned precariously back against an oak sapling, chewing on a straw, hands laced behind his head, responded to Woodard's observation.

"That's true, Woodard, but I kinda like that new fellow Shumpert. I didn't much approve of the way Corley handled that murder affair with old Mr. Asbill out at Fairview. Seems to me he kinda swept the facts under the rug because it didn't involve any of the town folks. Never even arrested anyone to my knowledge, even though the evidence was pretty substantial on those two Gardener boys I heard."

While the men-folk talked politics, the women discussed matters of importance to them: childrearing, cooking and sewing. They had no part in the politics, no vote. The only influence they had, if they even had an opinion, had to be funneled through their husbands. Women never expressed political views in public, only to their husbands in private.

After a short spell, Kel and his son Kelly walked up, carrying the children. Leon began to wiggle in his granddaddy's arms. He was ready to get down and see what he could get into.

"Put him down here, Pa, by Nina Lee," Corrie said. "I'll keep an eye on both of them."

"You better keep a watchful eye on Leon, Corrie. He will get into trouble before you can snap your fingers," responded Kelly. "That boy was messing around over by the washstand in the kitchen yesterday and managed to turn a whole bucket of water down on his head. Coughed and wheezed, practically drowned himself." They all laughed at Leon's misadventure as Kel sat the youngster on the grass at Corrie's feet.

It was quite a celebration, with neighbors milling around laughing and talking with each other and music in the background. Small groups stood everywhere, commenting on the coming election, anticipating the food, and complimenting Abe Hall and all those that donated their time to the preparations. Kelly and his brothers got quite a few compliments on their building a fine-looking platform. And it did look so patriotic with the red, white and blue draped across the front. Little groups of men talked quietly about the drinking of last evening and hoped that there would be no problems today.

"I see those Hall brothers, Little Jim and Samson, are back,"

Kelly announced to Roston, Sam, and Woodard. "I would hate for them to cause a ruckus and force us to whip their asses in front of the whole crowd. Sorry about the language, ladies, but I can't help getting riled up thinking about the trouble those two caused last night."

"They'll be ok, Kelly, I think," said Sam. "I haven't seen them disappearing over to their wagon to refill but once. They're pretty good boys when they have their wits about them. But we'd better keep a watchful eye on them just the same; they can get mean when they're drunk. I think I'll just mosey on over and visit with them and size up the situation; might have me a little drink myself." Sam began to walk away from his brothers in the direction of the Halls.

"Wait up, Sam, I'll go with you," called Woodard.

Dismissing the presence of the Halls, Roston stated. "Mr. Joe Gantt has his photographic equipment all set up over behind the platform Kelly. Don't you want to have a picture made of you, Mary, and the chaps?"

"Yes, I would like to have a likeness of Mary and the children taken before we leave." Directing his gaze towards his wife, he briefly shrugged his shoulders in question. Nodding in the affirmative, Mary rose with Louise, took Leon's hand, and followed Kelly towards the photographer.

At precisely 11:00 o'clock, the honorable Colie L. Blease, governor of the great state of South Carolina, arrived in a chauffeur driven Model T Town car. It was hard to say what was more impressive to the folks, Governor Blease or the car. Governor Blease immediately began working the crowed, shaking hands and kissing babies. He was a popular man in the state and practically a neighbor to the folks at the barbeque today. After all, he was a favorite son of the adjoining county of Newberry and no stranger to a lot of the people present. He had been elected unopposed in November 1910 and was sure to have a similar victory in November 1912. It's kind of hard to lose an election when you have no competition. He thought it prudent, never the less, to campaign and make a good showing on Election Day.

At quarter to twelve, Abe Hall stepped up onto the platform, thanked all the good folks and their honorable guests for coming. Then the pastor of the Steadman Baptist Church returned thanks for the food and good fellowship of the day. After a communal and loud 'Amen,' dinner was served.

Their guests went through the line first, then the men-folk, and lastly the women with their children hovering beside them. The mothers helped their small children by fixing their plates; the older children fixed their own. The crowd sat in small groups under the shady trees and the shed holding plates piled high with barbeque and fixings. After folks had their fill of the main course, they descended on the dessert tables and completely stuffed themselves.

By two o'clock, the crowd was somewhat more subdued. They sat in the shade on blankets and chairs visiting, but the laughter was not as loud and boisterous. Everyone was full of good food and the heat was beginning to slow their enthusiasm. The women-folk did their job of clearing the tables and packing up the remaining food while the men sat in groups, talking and fanning away the insects. The laughter of the children splashing at the edge of the pond under the watchful eyes of their mothers or older siblings resounded in the background. It was time now for the visiting politicians to take to the platform and solicit support for their election or reelection, as the case may be.

* * * * *

The first speaker was, of course, the Honorable Governor Blease. He began by telling a few simple jokes to draw smiles and laughter from the crowd. "It sure is an honor and pleasure to be here among you folks today. And I must say, that was the best barbeque pork I have had in recent memory. To you ladies, I have never known one community to produce so many fine cooks. It was a real enjoyable meal and I hope to be invited back next time you folks have a fourth of July celebration. You all know what I stand for and why I hope you will vote for me as your Governor again come November. Working for the good people of South Carolina has been my only concern, and I will continue to work in Columbia for all of you. Thank you most humbly for your support." He took his seat amid a wave of applause and a standing ovation from all those who were seated.

Roston leaned towards Kelly. "At least he kept it short and sweet, even if it was a bunch of bull."

The state legislators took their turn. Just more of the same: compliments and devotion for the work they hope to accomplish as servants of the people. When Thaddeus Corley and Willie Shumpert spoke to the crowd, everyone seemed to pay closer attention. Here at least there was some competition, and the office of sheriff was more important to these people's lives. They both spoke out against the unlawful practice of making moonshine; Shumpert especially spoke vigorously against moonshining, promising a more serious crackdown on the production. His strict stance elicited some boos from the back of the crowd. Of course, folks knew it was illegal and expected the sheriff to oppose the practice. but he didn't have to make it his main platform.

"Well I guess you're right, Woodard. Looks like Corley will get reelected," said Roston. "Too many folks in this neck of the woods make moonshine and won't vote Shumpert into office. Corley so far pretty much leaves us alone to our own business. Sure, his deputies sneak around and destroy a still now and again, but Shumpert sounds like he would really crackdown on the enterprise."

By four, the speakers had made their pitch to the crowd and the governor had departed. The men stood around, still hashing over what the candidates had said and questioning the ones still present. Many families began to pack their belongings, load up their children, and by five o'clock were headed towards home. They had livestock to see to and fussy children to contend with. It had been an enjoyable day and there had been no further trouble with regard to drinking, even though most all the men in the crowd had a snort or two from the bottle. It had been a memorable fourth for all the folks of the community.

Twelve

AT CHRISTMAS TIME IN 1912, CYRUS CAME HOME TO VISIT all his folks at Rayflin. He arrived on the 'Swamp Rabbit' one morning, three days before Christmas. None of the family knew he was coming; it was a complete surprise when the train stopped beside the railroad shack and a passenger stepped down. Roston and Kelly were in the store when the creak of the door swinging inward announced a customer. Cyrus appeared in the doorway just as Roston, behind the counter, glanced up from reading his paper. Kelly was sitting beside the wood heater with his back to the door.

"Good Lord, it's Cyrus!" Roston exclaimed as he stepped from behind the counter. Kelly rose and turned to face his older brother. They all embraced and gave each other a pat on the back.

"You are a sight for sore eyes, Cyrus!" Kelly exclaimed. "Does Ma know you're here?"

"Not yet, I guess I better get on up to the house and surprise her. I have been away for nearly two years and I thought it about time I came home to see for myself what my brothers were up to. The store looks good—how is business?"

"Pretty good, Cyrus," Roston answered. "How would you like a little drink to celebrate your return home?"

"Leave it to you, Roston, to offer a drink first thing. I better get on to the house and let Ma and Pa know the prodigal son is home first. I'll be back a little later to take you up on that offer and we can catch up on things," Cyrus replied as he headed out the door.

"It sure is good to see Cyrus again," Kelly said as the door closed behind him. "Ma is just going to be beside herself at the prospects of having all her children under the same roof for Christmas."

"I have an idea—why don't we just have ourselves a game of cards here in the store tonight?" asked Roston. "It is Saturday night and we brothers haven't played together in a long time. We'll have to wait until Rion and Buck are asleep or you know they'll have a fit to be included, and Ma wouldn't have that. Do you think Mary would be too upset if you spent the evening here and celebrated with your brothers?"

"Well, Mary won't like it, that's for sure, but I'll square it with her when I go home for supper. She's not unreasonable and she'll understand when I tell her Cyrus is home."

* * * * *

At around eight that evening, the brothers Roston, Cyrus, Kelly, and Woodard met at the store. Roston had a big fire going in the wood stove and had set up a table nearby with heavy oak chairs surrounding it. There was jug of moonshine sitting in the middle of the table to be passed around among the players. There was a spittoon nearby to spit their tobacco juice and two ashtrays on the table for those who would rather smoke while drinking and concentrating on their cards.

"Where is Sam?" Kelly asked.

"Oh, he'll be along after a while," replied Roston. "I saw him heading up the road towards Emma's. He's been sneaking up there to see her after Ma goes to bed. I don't think he's serious about her, just enjoys her company, if you know what I mean. I would bet my last dollar he's not reading poetry to her; it's something more physical, I grant you. I think he's spent the night up there with Emma a time or two, but he won't tonight; he's too fond of playing cards. He'll be here, you'll see."

"Did Mary give you a hard time about our little game, Kelly?" Cyrus asked.

"No, I just told her a man needs a little time and entertainment with other fellows now and again," Kelly replied. He made it sound as though there was no discussion when he told her what he intended to do. In reality, he wasn't nearly as firm as he led his brothers to believe. He pleaded with her not to be upset about the card playing and drinking and told her he would be home early. She didn't believe this, of course. She knew he would arrive home 'drunk as a skunk,' probably around sunup, and she would have to put him to bed. But she hadn't argued with him, knowing it was a useless cause; he would go just the same. And Mary knew he wanted to spend time with his brothers, so she held her tongue.

* * * * *

Sam had gone to see Emma Jeffcoat. Emma and her widowed mother, Mary, lived about two miles east of Rayflin on the road towards Pine Grove church. Mary's husband, Charlie Weaver Jeffcoat, had been a mean man and an outlaw. He had treated Mary cruelly and stopped by to see her only whenever he could stay ahead of the law. He had been involved in more than one bank robbery and even committed murder. A law man over in Aiken County had killed him in a shootout during a bank robbery attempt two years before. Mary didn't really miss her husband. Neighbors had always been able to tell when he was home to visit her. Mary would be sporting a black eye and bruises from a beating he had given her. Mary had gone to see her sister, so Sam and Emma had the place to themselves.

Sam was in the bed with Emma in the far corner of her old one room house when someone tapped on the door. "Mary... Mary... are you there?" the visitor whispered from outside the door.

"Emma, that's Pa, sure as hell! I better go tell him Mary's not here," Sam said. "I always suspected he was sneaking around seeing Mary, now I'm sure." Sam got up from the bed and tiptoed to the door. "Pa, Mary's not here," he whispered through the door.

"This ain't me, Sam," Kel replied. Then he abruptly turned and headed back to Rayflin.

Around ten p.m., Sam arrived at the store. The card game was going strong and after two hours of passing around the jug, everybody present was feeling pretty fine.

"Have you been up to see Emma?" Roston asked.

"Sure have, she is a real sweet gal and her ma was gone tonight, so we had no interruptions. At least not until Pa came tapping on the door."

"Pa? Are you kidding Sam?" Roston exclaimed.

"No, I'm not kidding; you know we talked about Pa maybe sneaking up there to see Mary. I told you Emma had hinted at it but never came right out and told me it was Pa."

"Well, what happened?" the brothers all asked in unison.

"Oh nothing, I just went to the door and said, 'Pa, Mary ain't here.'"

"And what was his reply?" Kelly asked.

"Evidently, he recognized my voice through the door. He said, 'Sam, this ain't me,' and then he was gone."

They all nearly 'bust a gut' laughing at their pa's reply to Sam.

"Don't be laughing so hard. You know if Pa finds out I told, he'll beat the hell out of me, and y'all too if you so much as mention it. If Ma finds out, there will be hell to pay."

The card game was interesting but by the time it broke up, the brothers were pretty much soused and couldn't actually remember who had won. Kelly did finally get home around three a.m., feeling real fine except for the problem of getting up the steps onto the front porch. Mary got up from her bed to help him inside and then unhitched the mule and put her in the barn.

"Kelly Gantt, I'm just glad you don't behave like this every night. Danged if you wouldn't have to sleep on the porch. I wouldn't be helping you to bed every night," Mary told him as she tucked him in. Of course, he didn't hear a word she said.

Next morning, Kelly got out of bed apologizing for his behavior and thanking Mary for taking care of him in his drunken state. Then he left for Rayflin to help Roston in the store. Business had been pretty brisk the last week or so with the local folks preparing for Christmas. Cyrus, Kelly, and Roston were in the store around

11:00 that morning when their pa walked in. Sam was nowhere to be found. He understood he should have kept his mouth shut about Kel interrupting him and Emma last night. He knew Roston too well and his weakness for gossip and telling everything he knew.

"How's business this morning, boys?" their pa asked.

"Oh, just fine, Pa," replied Kelly. "After Christmas, we're going to have to do a pretty big order to restock. We've been real busy the last couple of weeks."

"That sure is good news. I'll tell your ma at dinner. She'll be pleased to hear that too."

Kelly glanced over at Roston; he had been unusually quiet behind the counter. He noticed the grin on Roston's face and thought, *My God, he's going to say something we'll all regret.*

Sure enough, Roston just could not help himself. "I hear, Pa, Mary's over visiting her sister."

Kel's face turned beet red. There was no mistaking what Roston was referring too. *Damn that loudmouth Sam.* He turned slightly to face Roston, reached down, picked up one of the heavy oak chairs, and raised it over his head. "I don't give a damn if you are thirty-something-years-old and living on your own, I will still whip your ass," Kel said as he lunged towards Roston. "I will break this damn chair over your stupid head if you don't keep a civil tongue." Roston was out the door and gone before his pa could reach him, but the chair hit the door and shattered. Kelly and Cyrus didn't say a word; they had better sense.

"And you two better talk to that trifling brother of yours. He better keep his damn mouth shut if he doesn't want to tote an ass whipping. Do you have any idea what kinda hell your ma will dish out to me if she finds out? And y'all better be sure Roston understands and so do you," Kel said as he departed.

"Don't worry, Pa, we'll make it clear to Sam and Roston. They'll not say a word to Ma and neither will we," Kelly managed to get out before his pa left. As soon as Kel was out of earshot, Kelly turned to Cyrus and said, "That old man can sure get riled up. I thought steam was going to come out of his ears. I swear. that Roston can't keep nothing to himself. We better have a long talk with that boy."

* * * * *

Christmas was a joyous occasion. No more was said about their pa's infidelity, but Roston and Sam pretty much steered clear of him for the next two weeks. Peninnah didn't find out, not from any of her sons at least. If she had an inkling of the episode, no one ever knew.

After two weeks at home, Cyrus left Rayflin to return to his turpentine still in Alabama. He climbed aboard the 'Swamp Rabbit' one morning with the promise to write his ma and pa and the offer of a job to Roston and Kelly. But Roston couldn't leave his store and Kelly had a family to consider.

"I could sure use your help, little brother," Cyrus told Kelly before he departed. "And I would be willing to pay you five dollars a day, maybe a little more, if you're interested. I could sure use a good man I can trust."

"That's mighty generous, Cyrus. But I just can't see my way clear to leave Mary and the children now," Kelly said.

"If you change your mind, just drop me a line and catch the next train heading west. You'll have a job waiting whenever you want it," Cyrus replied. With a wave of his hand from the train window, he was gone. The 'Swamp Rabbit' moved down the track heading to Batesburg, through Georgia, and westward back to Alabama.

Thirteen

IT WAS JUST A MATTER OF TIME UNTIL IT HAPPENED: A CON-
frontation between Little Jim and Samson Hall and the Gantt
brothers. The Hall boys had not forgotten about Roston and Sam
escorting them home from the Fourth of July barbeque at the request of Brother Kelly. They were not the sorts to carry a grudge; in
fact, they had shared several drinks since with one or more of the
Gantts. But when they had been drinking a lot, they tended to get
ornery.

The following year in late July, the weather was hot and sticky,
escalating what otherwise might be a minor conflict. The confronta-
tion between the Gantt brothers and the Hall boys came to a head.

Little Jim and Samson had spent a day in Batesburg drinking
with a couple of buddies. They had actually gone to Batesburg to
pick up some medicine for Jim's mother, Miss Florence. Jim was a
good fellow when he wasn't drunk, and so was Samson. When Little
Jim got to drinking, he wanted to converse with anyone who would
listen about topics he didn't know a lot about. The booze inadvert-
ently made him feel smarter than he really was. The Halls lived right
up the road to the east of Rayflin with their parents, Florence and
Big Jim. Their father, Big Jim, farmed a fair amount of acreage with

the help of his two sons, but he had no control over their drinking. Late on this July afternoon, heading home, pretty well liquored up, they approached the turn-off for home and made the unwise decision to ride on down to Rayflin to see what the Gantts were doing; maybe they'd have another drink before heading home. They had heard Roston sold some powerful cider and wanted to try some.

As Little Jim and Samson passed the house at Rayflin, they saw Kel and Penninah sitting on the front porch enjoying the evening breeze before supper. Both the Halls waved in greeting and continued on down to Roston's store, where they knew some of the brothers would be.

"We'll just have a friendly drink of Roston's cider with the boys and buy us some smoking tobacco," Samson said. "Then we better be getting on home; it's close to supper time."

They pulled the horse and buggy to a stop between Roston's house and the store and gingerly climbed down. They were both pretty tipsy from the drinking and were not too surefooted.

When they entered the store, Roston was just lighting the kerosene lamps on both counters. It was still good daylight, but the light in the store was almost gone. Kelly, Sam, and Jule Smith, Corrie's husband, sat around a table in the center, talking.

Jule Smith got along well with his brothers-in-law for the most part. He was a pleasing fellow and loved his booze just like Corrie's brothers. He had, however, been known to be dramatic and stubborn, which eventually got him into trouble. All in all, Jule fit in well with the boys.

They were having a drink poured from a bottle Roston kept under the counter but were nowhere near as drunk as the Halls. Little

Jim and Samson were both in their twenties, young fellows but old enough to know deep subjects and strong drink don't mix.

"Well, how are you two fellows doing this evening?" Roston said. "What can I do you for?"

"We need to buy a can of that Prince Albert you have on the shelf," said Samson.

"And we could sure use a drink of that cider you keep there on the counter, Roston," Little Jim said, swaying and slurring his words as he took a seat opposite Kelly. "We been told its pretty good stuff."

"Sure thing, boys." Roston gave Samson the tobacco and Samson paid.

"How about that cider, Roston, before we go?" asked Little Jim.

Roston reached across and filled two small glasses from the cider keg sitting on the counter, pouring Samson and Jim a drink.

"Aren't you boys going to join us?" Little Jim posed to the others present.

"As soon as we finish what we have, we'll be glad to have another," Kelly replied. Kelly had just stood up and was busy sweeping the floor, anticipating closing up soon.

They shared a drink and some pleasant conversation for thirty minutes or so about their crops and the store business. Then Little Jim, in his drunken state, started talking about the Bible and his thoughts on the subject. Kelly, Sam, and Jule wanted no part of this conversation. Roston acted interested; he knew how Little Jim could be when he was drunk and didn't want to rile him up.

Little Jim got to talking about the stories described to him by the preachers he had heard; he, of course, had never read the Bible himself, but in his present inebriated state felt he knew more than he did. "Do you reckon all those plagues really happened to the

Israelites in Egypt? That business about the Red Sea becoming dry land so they could pass through that is hard for me to believe."

"You just have to have faith and believe what the Bible says," Roston replied.

"I know all about what the Bible says and how everything in it is supposed to be completely true, but some of the stories those 'hell and brimstone' preachers tell us might not be the gospel. Don't you think they tell us a lot of things just to scare the hell out of us? How do they know what really happened? Most everybody that reads the Bible understands it differently. Hell, most of it doesn't make good sense." Of course, his efforts to carry on a conversation were hampered by his slurred speech.

"Well, Jim, I believe, according to the Bible, what happened to the Israelites is true," Roston answered. "You just have to have faith; that's the main requirement."

"What about that, Kelly, do you believe it?" Little Jim asked.

Kelly's mind had been a thousand miles away and he had not an inkling of what Little Jim was talking about.

"Sorry Jim, what did you say?"

"I was talking about the Bible and those Israelites and all the plagues God tested their faith with in Egypt," Jim said. "All that business preached by them 'hell and brimstone' preachers we hear, do they know what in the hell they're talking about?"

"Jim, I don't think you or me either one is in a position to be talking about the Bible," replied Kelly.

"I know, Kelly, you have an opinion. Every one of us has been raised to believe in what the Bible says. What I want to know is do you believe the Bible is true? Yes or no, it's as simple as that to my way of thinking."

"Well Jim, I'm sure I don't know," replied Kelly.

"And I think you are a God damn liar, Kelly Gantt. I know you have an opinion."

Kelly ignored the swearing from Jim the first time, knowing he was completely drunk and was a different person sober, but then Jim made the mistake of calling Kelly a *God Damn Liar* a second time.

As soon as Little Jim swore at Kelly again, that did it. Kelly dropped the broom, grabbed Little Jim by the collar of his shirt, and hurled him out the open door of the store. That's when Samson jumped to his feet.

"What in the hell do you think you're doing, Kelly, throwing Jim out the door!" yelled Samson. "I reckon you boys are planning on escorting Jim and me home again. We won't go so peacefully this time."

Normally Kelly was a peaceable man, but Little Jim had tried his patience to the limit, he had been drinking too, and he wasn't about to take any mouth from Samson. "I ain't having no lowdown drunk calling me no G-D liar and if you know what's good for you and that loudmouthed brother of yours, you'll climb back in that buggy and head home. If not, I believe we can send you on your way and there won't be no escorting this time."

That was not a good enough response for Samson. He took a swing at Kelly and then a fracas did ensue. Samson was hurled out the front door behind his brother. Jule, Sam, Roston, and Kelly followed them to take the fight outside—no sense in breaking up things in the store. That's when Jim got to his feet and pulled a hawk billed pruning knife from his pocket, waving it menacingly at Jule. Jule, in his haste to back away from his antagonist and the extended knife, got his feet tangled up in some boards, stumbled, fell backwards to the ground. Jim was on top of him in a flash and cut Jule from the back of his neck all the way around to his nose.

Jule started yelling, "I'm killed! I'm killed!"

Kelly and Sam got a hold of Little Jim, pulling him off of Jule, and cut him up bad with their own knives.

Fortunately, Little Jim's knife was dull and didn't cut deep into Jule's neck, only deep enough to cause a profusion of blood. When Sam and Kelly released Jim, Samson helped him up and got him into the buggy. Jim was cut and slashed all over most of his upper body. He was bleeding like a 'stuck hog' by the time Kelly and Sam were done with him. That's when Kelly pulled his pistol from his pocket.

"Kelly, don't you shoot into that buggy," Roston said in an authoritative voice. "You'll be making a big mistake, and those two aren't worth spending time in jail."

"Take that damn brother of yours and get the hell out of here," Sam said to Samson, "before you get more of the same."

All this time, Jule had been screaming, "I'm killed, I'm killed."

Kelly checked Jule out and saw the wound wasn't deep; Jim's knife was too dull to cause much damage.

"Just shut the hell up, Jule," Kelly said. "You're not hurt badly, just a long scratch with a dull knife."

Jim and Samson pulled the buggy out into the road, Samson had the reigns. He pulled up in front of the store and stopped for a brief moment. He had a pistol under the buggy seat and decided if he was going to pull it out, now was the time.

While the Halls were leaving, Arthur Moore came up behind Sam and handed him his pistol. Arthur had borrowed Sam's pistol to take with him over to Tabernacle Church where the black folks attended service. Evidently Arthur felt like he might need it there, and anticipating the Halls unwillingness to leave, slipped up to Sam and returned his pistol. Sam stood in the door, his pistol in hand aimed at Samson. Samson stepped onto the running board of the buggy with his own pistol, but Sam had the drop on him.

"I wouldn't do that if I was you," Sam said.

Seeing the goings-on down at the store, their pa Kel walked up.

"Hell, I think I'll just kill you anyway, you sorry bastard!" Sam exclaimed. "Then we won't have to deal with you and that trifling brother of yours any more. He'll know to stay away."

Kel shoved Sam just as the pistol discharged and the bullet hit the dirt. Samson, needing no further encouragement, slapped the reins on the mule's back; they were gone.

"I just be damned, you boys let them Halls come down here and beat the daylights out of all of you," Kel said. "Just look at you, bruised and bloody, and there were only two of them."

"Pa, you don't know what in the hell you're talking about," said Kelly. "You don't reckon they got any scratches." And they all disappeared inside the store, leaving Kel outside.

Two days later, Dr. Timmerman from up at Batesburg stopped by Kelly's house. "I had to sew Little Jim Hall up night before last, took a lot of stitches and he had lost an awful lot of blood. He still only has a 50-50 chance of pulling through," Dr. Timmerman stated. "What in the hell were you and Little Jim doing down at Rayflin? He could still die because of the loss of blood."

"Well, to be honest doc, I don't give a damn is he does die, sorry bastard."

"Kelly, this kind of foolishness needs to stop."

"I can't agree with you more, Doc, but those Halls came down there looking for a fight and they got it. They best not mess around at the store with their big talk. Me and my brothers are law-abiding, but we won't take any mouth off them Halls when they come down there drunk and swearing. Jim called me a God damn liar, not once but twice. I wasn't about to put up with the drunk bastard talking to me like that in my own place of business. I will, however, have a talk with the brothers about using knives when we can just as well beat the hell out of them with our fists. The best thing them two can do is stay the hell away from our place of business. If you go back to check on Jim again, you're welcome to pass that message along to the sorry rascals."

Kel also had a few words with his boys about the knives that evening. "I understand Little Jim was cut up pretty bad the other night. Next time, I think you boys just better confine your fighting to fists and leave them knives in your pockets."

"Pa, you're right about the knives but Little Jim could have done Jule real damage. Thank God that knife he was carrying was as dull as his wits. You know, carrying a dull knife is like carrying a gun with no ammunition," Kelly said. "It ain't worth a damn."

After the incident with the Halls, no more was seen of them for a while. In October, Kelly, and all the family were at Pine Grove Church for a Revival meeting one night. The Halls were there. After the meeting, Little Jim, walked up to Kelly and said, "Can I have a private word with you behind the church?"

Kelly was leery of being out of sight with Little Jim. He didn't trust him or his motives.

"Ok, Jim, would it be all right if Rion came too?"

"Sure," Jim replied. They walked behind the church building.

"I just wanted to apologize for my behavior down at Rayflin. I was too drunk and didn't want that to come between us. We have been friends too long. Will you accept my apology, Kelly?"

"Apology accepted," said Kelly. They shook hands and no more was said about the episode. They remained friends for the rest of their lives and shared many a drink and conversation. They just never discussed Biblical teachings again.

Fourteen

IN AUGUST 1914, ALL OF EUROPE WENT TO WAR. TO THE Gantts at Rayflin, it might as well have been a million miles away. It was all so complicated. Peninnah would read from the newspapers brought to the Gantts on the 'Swamp Rabbit' around the kerosene lamp after supper was finished. The boys seemed interested, but Germany was on the other side of the world, thousands of miles away; it didn't seem to have any effect of their farm in rural South Carolina. After the newspapers were read at Rayflin, Kelly would bring them home and Mary would read them beginning to end.

She and Kelly would discuss the news articles and try to figure what was going on with the Germans.

"From what I understand from all that I have read," Mary explained to Kelly one evening, "the chain of events started when German armies invaded Luxemburg and Poland on August 2, 1914, then Belgium on August 4. Germany declared war on England and Russia, then Austria, Serbia, Italy, Rumania, Greece, Canada, and China got involved in the fight. I'm not sure who is actually fighting who, but it is clear the Germans started the whole mess. It truly can be described as a World War with so many countries already involved. The United States hasn't gotten involved yet. They have declared themselves neutral, but that won't last long. They'll eventually get involved, just wait and see," Mary stated.

Kel and Peninnah tried to keep abreast of the goings on in Europe too, but the newspapers delivered by train were usually at least a week old, so they had no up-to-date news. Kel, however, realized there was a high probability that America would not be able to stay neutral long and his crops would be in demand. If Americans didn't get in the fight with soldiers, they would surely back the war effort with supplies.

"We'll plant more wheat and corn, and of course cotton; that will be needed for uniforms, tents, and such," Kel remarked to Peninnah one morning. "I just pray we don't have to send Americans over there to fight."

"I hope we don't. Our boys are the right age to be soldiers, and that really worries me," Peninnah replied.

* * * * *

In November 1914, a man by the name of Wilbur Jones stopped by Kelly's. Wilbur was a representative of the Pond Branch Telephone Company, which was founded in 1909. He explained to Kelly that his company wanted to bring their service to folks in the community.

"The Pond Branch Company is willing to run the phone lines if landowners would put up their own poles. The phone itself could be purchased from the company for $4.75 and the customer would be responsible for a monthly bill of $2.75 for their service.

Would you consider signing up, Mr. Gantt?" he asked Kelly. "Your Pa, Mr. Kel, has signed up already," Wilbur told Kelly. "He says he and your brothers can get the poles up on the place this winter. Would you be interested in having a telephone installed here at your house?"

"I guess I will," replied Kelly. "How will the lines be running?"

"The line will start at Chalk Hill mine, cross the river at Rayflin to Mr. Kel's, by Pelt Branch up here to your house, then Northeast to Mr. Jimmy Gunter's, up Sweet Gum Bottom to the Asbill place, and into Steadman. We'll have a small office at Steadman and an operator on duty to connect the folks when they want to place a call."

"That sounds like a fine idea. I'll talk to Pa and we'll start getting them poles up right away."

"Good. Rhett Caughman or I will be here to supervise the placement and in a couple of months, y'all will have telephone service," Wilbur said, "and we do appreciate your business."

That evening at supper, Kelly explained to Mary all about the telephone lines and how they would be able to call down to Rayflin and talk to his ma and pa from their house.

"That sounds mighty exciting Kelly. Will I be able to talk to Sister Peggy? She's had a telephone at her house for several years and it would be wonderful to talk to her without having to take the train to Batesburg."

"Sure you can, Mary, maybe you can call her at least once a week to check on your pa and get the news."

"Speaking of news, Kelly, I may as well go ahead and tell you mine. You're going to be a father again. I've been real sick in the mornings lately and I know that can only mean one thing: I'm pregnant."

"That's good news Mary. And it doesn't make a mind to me what we have this time, a boy or a girl. Whichever will suit me just fine. When do you think we might be expecting this new baby?"

"Probably sometime in mid-June I figure."

"Speaking of children, where are those two little angels we have?" asked Kelly.

"They have already had their supper and are fast asleep. Leon is probably dreaming up some mischief to get into come daylight. He can think of more ways to get into trouble than any child I have heard tell of. Then he drags Louise in. He's the ringleader and she just follows his lead. Today they were playing in the parlor while I was in here cooking their dinner. They knew I was out of sight. One of them drug a chair over to the fireplace and Louise climbed up in it. When I realized how quiet they were, I snuck in there to check on them. Leon was kneeling on the hearth; Louise was standing in the chair and had gotten a box of matches from the mantle. She was handing Leon one match at the time; he would strike it and throw it in the fire. He kept saying, 'Hand me the box, Louise.'

"But not Louise, she would give him only one at the time to strike. I watched them for a few minutes and then cleared my throat. You should have seen Mr. Leon come up off that hearth and Louise get busy climbing off that chair. I tore both of their little behinds up. I can't leave them two alone for a minute."

* * * * *

"Leon's already has been in trouble playing with fire," Mary said. "I guess I forgot to tell you—remember when you bought your new pipe a couple of weeks ago."

"Yes, I do remember, left my old one on the kitchen mantle, as I recall."

"You did, and Leon climbed up there and got your old pipe and matches, went behind the outhouse, pulled some dry corn leaves twisted them together real tight, crammed them down in that pipe, and lit it. I was in the barn milking the cow, and when I came out, I smelled the smoke. The dried corn in the pipe must have been blazing six inches above the bowl, and he was trying to puff on that lit pipe. I said, 'Young man, just what do you think you are doing?'

"'Nothing Ma,' says Leon, but I saw him drop that pipe and cover it up with sand in the middle of that cornfield of dry stalks. 'Too late for you, young man,' I said and I tore his little backside up," Mary continued. "I thought he had learned his lesson and I explained to him he could have set the whole field on fire, but then I catch him and Louise with the matches, striking them in the parlor on the hearth. Try to keep matches in your overall pocket from now on; they can't be left out on the mantle, that's for sure."

"I'll have a word with Leon myself," said Kelly. "He could cause a major disaster if he gets his hands on matches again. I guess he thought he was mimicking me, but I need to sit a better example, especially with my pipe. Next thing you know, that boy will be chewing tobacco. Hey! Maybe it wouldn't be a bad idea to give him a little chew; it would make him sick as a dog, he'll be thinking he is falling off the world, might curb that desire to grow up so fast." Kelly couldn't help but laugh. "Sounds like you're right, Mary, Leon is a pistol alright. Kinda reminds me of some of the things my brothers and me use to think of that meant trouble. Ma tore our backsides up plenty of times; we sure didn't want Pa to find out about our shenanigans. He was a lot tougher than Ma. If he got a hold of you for some mischief, you made dang sure it didn't happen again. He was always rough on us when we were youngsters but fair. We deserved every lick we got."

Fifteen

IN THE WEEKS THAT FOLLOWED, KELLY AND HIS BROTHERS got busy setting the poles for the telephone lines. They started at the river, then through Rayflin across Kel's pastures and fields, passed Pelt Branch and Coon Branch to Kelly and Mary's house, then across the road to the boundary of Mr. Jimmy Gunter's land. Mr. Jimmy and his boys, Almon, John, and Reedy, placed the poles from there across their land. By planting time again, the lines had been run and telephones installed.

The telephone itself was a rectangular wooden box with a crank on the side. Two salmon-can-size batteries fit in the base and there was a detachable earphone on a cord. The speaker part was on the phone itself. There were no phone numbers; each person was allotted a ring tone, shorts and longs. Kelly's ring was two shorts and one long. Whenever the bell rung your assigned ring, you just picked it up and answered. Of course, everybody in the community heard it ring and most everybody listened in to your conversation, but the important thing was not to discuss matters that you didn't want everyone to know about. It was comforting for Mary to know if she needed Kelly when he was down at Rayflin, she could call him. Otherwise she wouldn't be using it except to talk to Sister Peggy, and she would let Kelly do the calling for her. She was a little leery of machines she didn't understand and she certainly didn't understand the concept of telephones even though Kelly had explained it. It was just hard to imagine sending your voice over phone lines and being able to talk to someone miles away. The first Saturday after the telephone was hooked up, Kelly placed a call to the Shealys in Batesburg so Mary could speak to Peggy. It was kind of complicated; first he had to turn the crank to connect to the operator, Gladys Hallman, in Steadman, and then Miss Gladys connected to the operator in Batesburg, who in turn rang the telephone at Peggy's.

"Ok, Kelly, you can go ahead now, I have Mrs. Shealy on the line," Miss Gladys said.

Kelly handed the phone to Mary and she and Peggy talked about fifteen minutes. Mary told her sister all about the children and they talked about their pa, Mr. Fink.

"I'm so glad Papa has that job with Tom, Peggy," Mary remarked. "When you get as old as Papa, keeping busy keeps you going and gives you a reason to get out of bed in the mornings. And I know he loves socializing with Tom's customers. Roston is like that at their store in Rayflin. He just loves to talk; Kelly does the finances and most of the ordering, but Roston is there to talk and gossip."

Peggy and Mary had a pleasant conversation but Mary didn't talk to Peggy about the one thing she wanted to: her pregnancy. Kelly had warned her that all the community could be listening to their conversation, and Mary knew pregnancy was one subject not to be discussed when prying neighbors were privy to your conversation. Mary really needed someone to unburden her frustrations about her condition. Someone who would sympathize about her struggle to just get out of bed in the mornings, how she had to grasp the iron headboard and pull herself up, then squeeze her swollen feet into her shoes. How drained and tired she felt by midafternoon, tending to two little children, cooking, cleaning, and taking care of the animals. How she climbed into bed every evening exhausted, unable to have a decent night's sleep because there was no way to get comfortable with her growing belly, just to wake the next morning and start all over. These were things she couldn't tell Kelly. She knew he would listen, but being a man, he wouldn't really understand. Besides, she wasn't a complainer and he had much more on his mind with spring almost here and crops to be planted.

Planting time was the busiest time for Kelly and all his family. They started in March preparing the fields for planting. By March twentieth, the corn was planted and in the month that followed, so were all the other crops: wheat, cotton, oats, peanuts, rye, and velvet beans. Both Mary and Peninnah also insisted on an acre for their vegetable garden. The women were in charge of the gardening, but the men-folk broke the ground up with their plows and sowed the seeds. This year, however, Mary was in no condition to do a lot of gardening. She insisted on helping, but at seven months pregnant, she wasn't able to squat beside a butter bean bush in the hot sun and pick beans or chop weeds from around the tomato plants. Peninnah and Jennie took care of the garden at Rayflin and at least one day a week came to help Mary with her garden.

Kelly had 40 acres he planted with cotton, corn, and wheat at his place with the help of the Burketts and Hardys. The Burketts lived in a four-room house about midway between Kelly's house and his pa's. Uncle Caesar and Aunt Maggie, so all the white folks called them, had five boys: Rufus, Liam, Hargo, Charlie and baby Willie. Their two girls, Jennie Lou and Sibbie, and Uncle Caesar's ma, Aunt Chaney, also lived with them. Aunt Chaney had married Alfred Gantt, but he had passed away some years before and so she lived with her daughter-in-law Maggie, her son Caesar, and their children.

The Hardys lived past Kel's place on the road to Sugar Bottom. Uncle Tom and Aunt Jane Hardy also had boys, Dave, Ab, and Joe, who helped with the planting both in Kelly's fields and at Rayflin. Arthur Moore also worked on the place and lived in a small two-room house just a hundred yards east of Kel and Peninnah's. Kelly was mainly a farmer like his pa. Of course, he did keep the books for Roston's store and had worked at sawmills and carpentry, but farming was what he really enjoyed. He had cleared his fields and built his house on the north section of his pa's place. He knew his inherited acreage would be in this section, but Kel had never made any legal papers to that effect. Kelly hated to mention his feelings to his pa. *Pa would think I didn't trust his word or that I was anticipating his demise,* Kelly thought. It did sort of cause ill feelings for him to know that this place he had put so much time and work into was not legally his.

By June, the crops on the place were doing fine. Rain had watered the fields at least two days a week when the plants needed it most in April and May. The corn was tasseling; the young ears were beginning to fill out, and the cotton plants were blossoming, requiring constant attention to keep the weeds chopped and under control. Mary's garden was bursting with a profusion of tender vegetables.

Early on Saturday, June twelfth, Mary grabbed two baskets and an old straw hat and headed to the garden down near the spring with Leon and Louise in tow. There were butter beans to pick, the first mess of the season and she wanted to get them picked before midday, when the heat would be unbearable. She couldn't wait for Jennie and Miss Peninnah to find the time to come help her. They had their own garden to worry about and she was quite capable, even though it would be awkward in her condition. Kelly was already in his fields with Ab and Dave Hardy, chopping cotton. If he knew she intended to pick the beans, he would insist on helping and Mary knew he had more pressing matters to be concerned with. Mary squatted down beside a row of butter beans and began picking the ones that were filled out enough to eat. Leon and Louise played at the end of the row in the shade of a large pecan tree. Mary glanced up every so often just to make sure they were where they were supposed to be. She needn't to have feared they would wander off; they knew Momma would tear their 'sit downs' up if they didn't obey. She was too close for them to think about misbehaving. By 9:00, Mary had a half-bushel basket of butterbeans picked, a dozen tomatoes, and a like number of squash. The tomatoes and squash were just beginning to come in, but there was more than enough for their supper. As she trudged up the incline to the backyard with her basket of beans, Leon and Louise followed, sharing the burden of the basket holding the squash and tomatoes. Mary intended to spend the next few hours in the shade on the porch swing shelling the butterbeans while Leon and Louise played in the yard under her watchful eye. Just as she reached the back steps and started up, a pain shot through her abdomen. Mary paused, grabbed her stomach, a frown furrowing her brow. *This could be labor,* she thought. *It's time for this baby to arrive.*

"Are you ok, Mamma?" Leon asked. "You sure had a funny look on your face."

"I'll be fine, Son," she replied as she held the screen door open for Leon and Louise to pass through with their basket. "We'll just put our baskets here on the table."

Another pain hit stronger than the first and Mary knew she had to make haste and get some help.

"Leon, do you think you could go to the cotton field and fetch your daddy while I rest a spell?"

"Sure I can, Momma," Leon replied. It made him feel awfully grown up to have his momma sending him on an errand. Usually she didn't let him out of her sight.

"You go straight there and find your daddy, no dawdling, you understand? Tell him I need him right away."

"Sure, Momma, I understand," Leon said as he pushed the screen door open and bounced down the steps.

Kelly knew something was wrong as soon as he spotted Leon running across the end of the cotton field. Leon tried to jump over the cotton rows, but with his short legs, every other step landed squarely on a cotton plant. Kelly dropped his hoe and ran to meet his little son.

"Momma says she needs you, come to the house right away," Leon managed to get out between gasps. The little fellow was so tired from running; Kelly bent down and scooped him up in his arms. Leon began to cry as they hurried towards the house.

"Don't cry, Son, I'm sure your Momma is fine. The baby is about to arrive, that's all and your Momma needs a little help to get it here."

"A baby?" Leon asked. "Is that all? I thought she was really sick."

When Kelly and Leon came in the back door, Mary was nowhere to be seen.

"I'm in here, Kelly," Mary called from their bedroom on the other side of the wall. Kelly hurriedly crossed the dining room, exited through the screen door onto the front porch, and entered the other part of the house. Mary was sitting on the edge of their bed; Louise had helped her mother remove her shoes and was fanning her with a cardboard church fan.

"You may as well call Miss Hannah, Kelly. This baby is coming soon," she said as a sharp pain hit and a little shudder enveloped her body.

Miss Hannah lived with her son, Jimmy Gunter, not a half mile away. Kelly made the call and talked to Mr. Jimmy. "Almon will bring Ma over right away, Kelly. Good luck on this new baby."

In less than thirty minutes, Miss Hannah arrived and Mary felt more at ease. She knew Miss Hannah could take care of things and everything would be all right now.

"Kelly, you get them two little ones out of here and I'll help Mary deliver them a little sister or brother."

Kelly and the children retired to the front porch along with Almon. He was six years younger than Kelly but they had always been good friends. Almon decided to stay to keep Kelly company; afterwards, he would take his grandma home.

They sat on the front porch, rocking and talking most of the afternoon while Leon and Louise played in the yard. Mary's afternoon was not as leisurely spent. Labor is hard no matter how many children you birth, but this being the third, things did progress much faster. At a little past three in the afternoon, the little group keeping vigil on the front porch heard the wail of a baby. Miss Hannah appeared shortly thereafter and announced the birth of a fine baby girl.

"Can we go see her now?" Leon and Louise asked in unison.

When Kelly, Louise, and Leon entered the bedroom, Mary lay smiling and holding a little bundle with a tiny head just visible above the covers. They gazed at their new sister with wonder shining in their dark eyes.

"But Momma," Leon said, "where is her hair?"

"She doesn't have any just yet, Son, but she will soon," replied Mary.

"What's her name?" Louise asked.

"Her name is Elsie Juanita Gantt. What do you think of that name, children?"

"It's fine with us, Momma, but can I just call her baby?" Leon asked.

"If you want to, Son," replied Mary. "I'm expecting both of you to help me take care of your little sister Elsie. Is that a bargain?"

"Sure, we'll help," they both replied.

"You might just be getting more help than you bargain for," Kelly laughed. "She is a pretty little thing. Now I have three little angels."

Sixteen

TWO WEEKS AFTER ELSIE'S BIRTH, MARY FELT IT WAS TIME for her to get back to her work, tending to children, cooking, and managing her household. Kelly had been a big help with Louise and Leon, fixing their breakfast every morning before he began work in his fields. He knew childbirth was hard on a woman and Mary needed some time to regain her strength—hadn't Miss Hannah and his momma told him so more than once?

Louise and Leon both dressed themselves as soon as their little feet hit the floor in the mornings. They would dress, peep in on their mother and baby Elsie, and then fly out the screen door, cross the front porch, and join their father in the kitchen, where they kept up a steady stream of conversation, a goodly portion of their chatter devoted to questions they expected him to answer.

"Daddy, what are you going to do today?" Louise asked. "Can Leon and I help you in the field?"

"Well, let's see, Louise. You answered your first question for me. I'll be working with Ab and Joe in the fields. And no to the second question; the answer is the same as it was yesterday and the day before. You and Leon have to stay here with your mother and Elsie."

"It would be more fun to go with you, Daddy, than to stay here with Momma," Leon stated in a matter-of-fact tone.

"I couldn't watch you two and do my work. You might wander off and get on a snake. Besides, your momma is depending on y'all to help her.

"She's too busy watching the baby to pay us any attention," Leon intoned with just a bit of jealous sarcasm. "How did baby Elsie get out of Momma's tummy anyway? I've been trying to figure that out."

Leon, being the more curious of the two children, had asked Miss Hannah, "Where did that baby come from? I don't understand."

"Of course you don't, young mister," she replied, not wanting to say things that the children would not understand. "When your daddy Kelly called, Almon and I stopped in the woods on the way over and found that precious little baby in a stump hole."

Leon told his daddy, "The next day, Louise and I searched the woods over looking for a baby. We were in a discussion about who was going to carry it to the house." The explanation Miss Hannah had given the children was more confusing than the truth. Grownups believed children would ask fewer questions if some outrageous explanation was given. After all, little children believed in magic and fairytales more than reality, and they both were satisfied, at least at the time. Leon, at five-years-old and Louise, at four, were more than happy to except Miss Hannah's answer. Since then, Leon, a bright child, had noticed that his mother's tummy had disappeared with the appearance of baby Elsie.

Kelly paused for a moment. "Son, I'll explain that to you in a few years. Now both of you eat your grits and stop asking so many questions. Y'all sure do a lot of talking first thing in the mornings."

Mary opened the screen door from the porch and entered the kitchen.

"It's about time I get back to my chores. I'm feeling pretty well this morning," she said as she bent and planted a kiss on both Leon and Louise's heads and a brief kiss on her husband's cheek.

"Don't be overdoing it, you hear?" Kelly said. "Elsie is only two weeks old; you still need to take it easy for a while."

"I will, I promise. Aunt Maggie and her girl, Sibbie, stopped by yesterday and she insist on sending Sibbie up here to help me with all these 'chil'uns,' as Aunt Maggie says. It would be nice to have some help for a few weeks in the garden and with the milking and cleaning. Can we pay Sibbie a couple dollars a week to help around here with the children and the chores?" Aunt Maggie said Sibbie wouldn't be needing no pay and not to even think about it, but I know they can use the money and right now I can use the help."

"Of course, we'll pay Sibbie. I wouldn't expect the child to come here and work for nothing. I'll have a word with Uncle Caesar and Aunt Maggie on the way to Pa's this afternoon. Otherwise, they probably wouldn't let her accept the money. They are two good people. I know they could use a little extra money and we can afford to pay her a few dollars."

Soon after Kelly departed for the fields, Mary and the children heard a sweet voice singing outside. "That sounds like a Sunday song, Momma. Is that an angel singing?" asked Louise.

"No, child, I think that is Sibbie coming up the road. She's going to help us out with chores for a few days. I expect you two to behave and not give her any cause to regret being here."

Sibbie Burkett was fourteen years old, tall and slim with gingerbread-colored skin. She was Uncle Caesar and Aunt Maggie's oldest girl. She had four older brothers who helped the Gantts in their fields and a younger sister, Jennie Lou, and younger brother, Willie. As soon as she stepped up on the porch and knocked on the screen door, Louise and Leon scrambled down from the table and were at the door to greet her.

"Good morning, Miss Mary," she said with a smile. "And how are you little children this morning?" She dropped her gaze, addressing Louise and Leon.

"We're fine," both children replied in unison, grinning up at the young girl standing outside the screen door.

"Do come in, Sibbie," said Mary, pushing open the screen. "Have you had your breakfast this morning?"

"Oh yes, ma'am, I have, about an hour ago. My ma doesn't believe in wasting daylight. Now, Miss Mary, I am here to help you with whatever needs to be done. I have tended to my little sister and brother and I do most of the cooking and cleaning for my ma, just tell me what you need done and I will be glad to get started."

"Well, Sibbie, I think we'll mostly need to work in the garden this morning. Since the baby has come, I haven't been able to pick the butterbeans, tomatoes or squash. I'm sure we have corn and cucumbers ready and all that needs to be picked. Kelly's Ma, Miss Penninah, and Jennie came by one day last week and gathered the vegetables but with the rain we had two days ago, I'm sure everything is ready again."

"Where is the garden? And I'll be needing your baskets," said Sibbie. "I'll get started right away."

"Sibbie, I don't expect you to do all the work by yourself. I would just appreciate some help for a few days."

"Yes'um, whatever you say I'll be glad to do."

Sibbie and Mary were soon down in the garden gathering butterbeans, corn, squash, tomatoes, and carrots. Elsie was asleep in her cradle and every fifteen minutes or so, Mary and Sibbie took turns trudging up the hill to check on her and make sure she was still sleeping.

Louise and Leon played in the shade while the women worked. They got all the vegetables picked and headed back up to the house. Sibbie, Leon, and Louise managed to carry the baskets; Sibbie insisted they were much too heavy for Mary to be carrying so soon after having a baby. Picking was the beginning of the process. All the vegetables had to be washed, the butterbeans shelled and washed before they could be cooked for their supper. Mary and Sibbie sat in the shade of the porch swing and shelled the butterbeans while Leon and Louise played in the yard.

Sibbie put the beans in water with a large slice of fatback. Soon, the beans came to a boil and the heat of the stove was decreased. The fire had burnt down and the beans could simmer on the woodstove without worry of scorching in the bottom of the pot. Mary continued to lift the lid to stir them and add water and small pieces of wood to the fire if need be. Maintaining a low simmer with a woodstove took practice and cooking expertise, which Mary had learned from her momma. She would continue to simmer the beans until supper time. Sibbie also washed the other vegetables for Mary. She was such a big help. Mary sat at the kitchen table slicing the tomatoes and squash. She felt she could finish the cooking now that Sibbie had done the biggest part of the work. When Sibbie left for the day, Mary would fill a basket with vegetables for Sibbie to take home to her folks; there were more than enough for both families.

After they worked in the garden, shelled the beans, and had them cooking, Sibbie took Leon and Louise up to the barn and took care of the animals, feeding the mules, cow and pigs. What chickens Mary had roamed free in the yard and were only let in their coop at night, the door closed to hopefully protect them from foxes. Kelly would see to that when he got home and would milk the cow. Sibbie had offered but Mary insisted that could wait until Kelly got to the house late in the evening.

By this time, the temperature began to cool and a slight breeze began to stir the tops of the chinaberries and magnolia in the back yard. Sibbie sat on the back steps and watched Leon and Louise play between the chinaberry trees. It was really pleasant and the children stayed where Sibbie told them to; it was almost relaxing for her just sitting on the steps.

While Sibbie was watching the two older children, Mary fed and changed Elsie then returned to the kitchen while she continued to monitor the beans. She lay Elsie on a pallet in the dining room where the heat from the cook stove would not be so bothersome to her, but she would be near enough that Mary could check on her often.

By suppertime, all the chores were done. Sibbie had been a real help to Mary. She never had to be asked twice to do anything. She was a good worker, quiet but with a sense of humor. She told Mary and the children stories about her family and funny things her brothers did. The children liked her immediately; she took time to answer their questions and didn't seem to mind how inquisitive they were about the color of her skin.

Sibbie left, heading home about five o'clock; she wanted to be there before the sun went down. The children watched her from the front porch walking with the basket of vegetables on her arm and humming a song. She turned once and waved, shouting, "I'll see you two bright and early tomorrow."

* * * * *

For the next two months, Sibbie worked for Mary and Kelly. She was there every morning during the week soon after breakfast and stayed until the chores were caught up and Mary had supper cooked. Leon and Louise looked forward to Sibbie's arrival every morning. Not only did she help Mary in the garden, she took the children with her to the barn in the afternoons when she went to feed the animals and sometimes milk the cow. She told Mary t'was no need for Mr. Kelly to have that chore when he had been in the fields all day.

The children both minded Sibbie pretty good, knowing one word from her to their mother about misbehavior and their backsides would be sore. Mary was strict when it came to her children. She was good to them and loved them but wouldn't put up with foolishness when it came to expected behavior.

One afternoon in late August, Sibbie, Louise, and Leon headed to the barn to milk the cow and feed the mules, chickens, and pigs. Leon had been especially defiant all day. Mary had already had to cut a keen switch and use it on his bottom for dumping a handful of sand on Louise's head and teasing her, making her cry, when they were playing in the backyard.

As they headed to the barn, Leon ran ahead and Sibbie had to yell, "Leon, wait up for me and Louise, don't be running ahead, and get down off that mule lot fence right this minute."

"Get down from there, Leon, before you fall," Sibbie repeated. "Your momma would be upset if you hurt yourself." Leon seemed determined to get himself into more trouble. The children knew they were not allowed in the stall when Sibbie milked their old red milk cow. She had been known to kick and it was too dangerous for the children to be near her. Sibbie went in, pulled up her stool, and began milking.

Leon crawled under the gate against Louise's protest. "Don't go in there Leon," Louise whispered, "it's too dangerous and you're going to get in trouble." Before Sibbie realized, he was standing behind the cow. She reached over, grabbed Leon's arm and pulled him out of the way just as 'old Bess' kicked the side of the barn.

"Get out of here right now, Leon; you could have been killed!" Sibbie screamed, visibly shaken by the event.

Leon was not in the least bit afraid. "That old cow missed me by a mile and you can't tell me what to do; you're not my momma!" he yelled to Sibbie.

"You're right about that, young mister. For one thing, I'm too young to be your Ma and for another my skin is the wrong color," replied Sibbie. "But you will mind what I say or I'll tell your momma and she can deal with you."

Leon clammed up immediately, realizing he had made a big mistake talking to Sibbie in that way. "I'm sorry, Sibbie, really, I am. I shouldn't have said what I said, please don't tell my momma."

"If you promise to mind me from now on, I won't tell her, but I better not have any more sass from you, young man. Do you understand?" asked Sibbie.

"I'll be good, I promise," Leon replied.

He was a perfect little angel the rest of the day. Sibbie didn't tell Mary about the incident. She didn't have too, Louise did and he got his backside switched again. After that, Sibbie had no more trouble with young mister Leon.

At the end of August, Mary felt she could take care of things on her own and told Sibbie she wouldn't need her to come every day. "I hate to let you go, Sibbie. You have been so much help to me with the children and chores around here. I don't think I could have managed without you."

"I understand, Miss Mary, but if it's ok with you, I'd like to stop by every so often and check on Leon and Louise. They're mighty sweet little children, even if they can be a bit rambunctious at times."

"You feel free to come visit anytime, Sibbie. You're always welcome."

Seventeen

"IN FALL OF 1915, THE EDISTO KAOLIN CO. BUILT A STORAGE shed at Rayflin. The storage shed was a simple structure with a log foundation: vertical 1 inch x 10 inches siding covered the three outside walls of the 20x40 foot shed. A covered platform ran along the open side next to the track and the roof was covered with 'roll roofing.' It was separated into five compartments with no doors between; the two compartments used for bulk storage had openings near the roof to allow dust to escape. The bulk kaolin was in fifty-pound paper bags and was like fine flour; the other kaolin brought to the shed was also bagged but in chunks. It was delivered to the shed at Rayflin twice a day in two mule-drawn wagons and once on Saturday." — Buchner Sr, *The Swamp Rabbit, Its Time, And Its People*

"The S&K Railroad at the request of Edisto Kaolin Company had constructed a sidetrack that would hold eight cars at Rayflin. The kaolin was stored here in the shed out of the weather until the 'Swamp Rabbit' delivered empty cars onto the sidetrack and enough kaolin was in the shed to fill the cars. Once the cars were loaded and ready to be shipped, the Swamp Rabbit picked up the cars and delivered them to Perry; from there it was transported to the coast at Savannah, Georgia." — Buchner Sr, *The Swamp Rabbit, Its Time, And Its People*

Kelly was employed by the Kaolin Company to help the Company men construct the storage shed, and their presence while working on the shed increased Roston's business at the store. After the shed was completed, the fellows that delivered the kaolin to Rayflin twice a day usually came by the store for a little refreshment. It was a slow, dusty three-mile ride in a mule-drawn loaded wagon from the mine to Rayflin, especially during dry weather.

All the Gantt brothers soon became well acquainted with the drivers that brought the kaolin. Roston had started selling hard cider he purchased from over near Wagener and it became a big favorite with the men from the mine. The cider keg sat on the far end of the counter surrounded by glasses; a glass of cider could be purchased for five cents. It was good stuff, but man, was it potent.

An old black fellow, Uncle Lewis Jerry, came into Roston's store one afternoon from the mine. He had just unloaded the last delivery of chalk for the day and came in for a little refreshment before heading on back.

"Mr. Roston, I've heard you sell some good cider at your place of business. I think I would like to try me a glass."

"Sure, Uncle Lewis, I will be more than glad to oblige, but remember that stuff is potent. It'll make a rabbit spit in a bulldog's face," replied Roston with a chuckle.

Well, Uncle Lewis got into the cider, drank four glasses, and by the time he left, he could hardly walk. Roston went out and helped the old man back up on the wagon.

"You sure you can make it back ok?" Roston asked.

"Why yes, Mr. Roston, I am just as fine as frog's hair," Uncle

Lewis replied, swaying as he untwisted the reins looped around a nail on the side of the wagon bench.

Roston stood outside the store and watched as Uncle Lewis started off in the wagon. Later that evening, as Roston was relating the story to all his customers in the store, he said, "Shaw, Uncle Lewis fell off the wagon down behind the mule before he even reached the river bridge. Good thing I saw him; he wasn't hurt, but me and Sam had to get him up and drive him and his wagon back to the chalk mine." There were many such incidents concerning Roston's hard cider, but it was sure a big seller.

* * * * *

The War in Europe was in full swing in the fall of 1915. German U-boats began their first campaign of submarine warfare aimed at Allied shipping the previous February, and in May of 1915, a U-boat sunk the Lusitania with the loss of some one hundred and twenty-four American lives. The United States was shipping supplies of food, armaments, and all manner of manufacturing goods to the allies in Europe and had brought pressure to bear on Germany to end sinking of shipping vessels without warning. In August of 1915, Germany prohibited this practice. Naval stores, the collective name for all products of the gum from pine trees, were in enormous demand throughout the world, especially in Allied Europe. Turpentine and rosin, the two byproducts of the gum, were used in the manufacture of paint, paper, and medicine, just to name a few. With the great demand, turpentine production was in full swing throughout the South.

The first of November 1915, Kelly received a letter from Brother Cyrus in Alabama pleading with him to come to Alabama and work for him at the turpentine still.

"I know you have a family to consider," Cyrus wrote, "but I can offer you $7.00 a day including Saturdays and you can room with me. If you could just see your way clear, come after Christmas; your planting time doesn't start until March. Even if you can help me out only a few months, that would be plenty of time for you to get my financial records in order and organized. You have always been good with financial matters; I don't really have the time or inclination to tackle the job myself.

"The sap doesn't rise until spring, but we have the dried sap to scrape from the 'cat faces' and pack in barrels to ship. Mainly I need you to straighten out my company books; they are in total disarray. I was never as good at figures as you are, please consider coming."

Kelly didn't show the letter to Mary right away. He did hate to leave her and the children alone. But the pay sounded mighty tempting; maybe if he went to Alabama and worked for Cyrus until spring planting, he could save enough money to buy that Model T he had wanted for so long. After carrying Cyrus's letter around in his breast pocket for a week, he decided it was time to talk to Mary.

The next week, he finally got up enough nerve to broach the subject. Mary and Kelly were sitting in the kitchen one evening. The children were all tucked into bed, the supper dishes were done, and they both sat at the table reading *The State* newspaper left by the Swamp Rabbit that morning. The paper was the November 6th edition, almost a week old. The lamp threw flickering shadows on the ceiling above and a small fire burned in the fireplace. It was almost their bedtime, and the fire had to burn down completely before it was safe to retire to bed and leave it unattended. There were still some leftover coals in the wood cook stove behind Mary, and the room felt nice and cozy, even though the wind could be heard as it howled outside and rattled the windowpanes.

"It must be really cold outside," Mary said. "Just listen to that wind, and the lower windowpanes are all steamy. I need to check on the children; they may need another quilt tonight."

"It is getting colder, I think," Kelly replied. "We might have some frost in the morning if this wind lies by midnight. It going to be near to freezing before daylight; I would venture to say."

"How was everybody down at Rayflin today?" Mary asked. "We really need to take the children down there come Sunday to see your pa and ma."

Kelly saw his opportunity as soon as Mary mentioned his family. It would seem only natural now to tell her about his brother Cyrus's letter.

"Oh, they're just fine. Pa is thinking about butchering a couple hogs soon. It's getting that time of the year you know. By the way, I received a letter from Cyrus in Alabama."

"And just how is your brother?" Mary asked. "It's seems like so long since he was here for Christmas. Did he mention coming for another visit?"

"Well, no, he didn't," was Kelly's reply, "but he's doing fine. The turpentine business is really booming with the War in Europe. He has a lot of fellows working for him and they are producing all the turpentine spirits and rosin they can to be shipped overseas. He asked me to come out there after Christmas and help him out about three months." There, he finally got it out. "He says he'll pay me $7.00 a day including Saturdays and I won't have any living expenses much. I can stay with him."

Mary stopped her reading and looked up into Kelly's eyes. Kelly couldn't read the expression in her eyes; the light from the kerosene lamp was too dim to reveal the feelings shadowed there. At first, she didn't reply and Kelly thought he would have to add more weight to his argument. When Mary finally did speak, she surprised her husband.

"Kelly, if you think you need to go, the children and I will be fine for a few months. That's awfully good pay, and we can certainly use the money. If you went right after Christmas, could you be back by middle of March when the planting starts? That's the only thing that would trouble me; I might have some trouble with the planting, but Ab, Joe, and Mr. Kel could handle things if need be. I'm sure Uncle Caesar and Aunt Maggie will let Sibbie come stay with the children and me. She could help out with the children and I wouldn't be so lonesome, having her to talk to in the evenings. We'll be fine, Kelly. It's your decision."

"Are you sure Mary? I hate like the devil to leave you and the children, but the money will be good. If you're sure you can get by without me for a few months, I'll go ahead and write to Cyrus and tell him to expect me after Christmas."

"I'm sure, Kelly. Go ahead and write your letter."

Eighteen

KELLY STOOD ON THE PLATFORM AT THE TRAIN STATION IN Augusta, Georgia. It was past three in the evening and he really needed to find himself some supper before the train for Atlanta, due at four o'clock, arrived. It was January 5th, 1916; he had left Rayflin on the Swamp Rabbit about eleven this morning, heading towards Batesburg. From Batesburg, he had boarded a freight train with only one passenger car heading west, crossed the Savannah River—the boundary between South Carolina and Georgia—around two p.m. and pulled into the station at Augusta.

Mary and the children had seen him off this morning. It had been a tearful farewell. Kelly had reminded Leon he would be 'the man of the house' while his daddy was gone. "Can you promise to take care of things at home, Son, and the girls while I am away?"

"I promise, Daddy, I will be a good boy and look after Momma, Louise and Elsie," Leon stated sternly. "You can depend on me, Daddy."

The morning seemed like a long time ago now to Kelly. He already missed his family and his journey had just begun. He knew he had no reason to worry about Mary and the children. His pa and brothers would keep a check on them and Sibbie had come to stay the afternoon before. Sibbie was dependable and levelheaded and would help Mary and give her someone to talk to. Kelly had never been any farther from Rayflin than Columbia, South Carolina's capital, never crossed a state line, and he had to admit, he had butterflies in his stomach.

I'm just too nervous to eat, he thought to himself. *I'm acting just like a schoolboy and I'm thirty-two years old. This is pure silliness. I'm a grown man just making a trip, not some schoolboy caught throwing spitballs.*

Kelly got on the train in Augusta at four-fifteen in the afternoon heading to the big city of Atlanta, Georgia. He sat next to a very nice gentleman going home to see his family, a Mr. Mosley who had been in Charleston settling his late father's estate. As the train rumbled towards Atlanta, Kelly stared out the window: the fields were barren and brown. Kelly saw fields of dried corn and bales of hay scattered haphazardly everywhere.

Pa would never have that on his place, Kelly thought. That hay would be stacked in a barn somewhere and the corn stalks would have been cut down months ago. Not everybody is as serious about their farming as Pa.

In the dimming afternoon light, they passed farmhouses standing as stark sentinels on the winter landscape. They did pass through small towns where passengers boarded and the train had to take on water, but Kelly left his seat beside the window only once when the train stopped in Athens, Georgia, north east of Atlanta. The train had a 30-minute stop here, so Kelly stepped down from the rail car just to stretch his legs and to smoke his pipe. When the train conductor shouted, "All aboard!" Kelly returned to his seat across from his new acquaintance, Mr. Mosley.

It's amazing what some people will tell perfect strangers. By the time the train reached Atlanta, Kelly would know personal details about Mr. Mosley and his entire family. Kelly was not that sort of person. Some things he felt too personal to share with just anybody, but not Mr. Mosley. Mr. Mosley's wife, Sara, had a drinking problem and his oldest son had been in trouble with the law. The conversation was interesting, however, and helped Kelly keep his mind occupied. By six p.m., it was dark and there was nothing for him to see from the train window so Mr. Mosley's conversation had been welcome.

The conductor came through and lit the kerosene lamps on the walls of their car before dusk settled over the countryside, but the lamps on either end of the car only produced a dim glow. It was hard to discern the facial features of those sitting near; Mr. Mosley's voice was almost comforting. When they finally reached Atlanta, it was almost four in the morning. The depot was well lit; Atlanta had electric lights, a marvel to Kelly since he wasn't used to this modern invention. Mr. Mosley's wife and son were at the depot to meet him even at this early hour. Mr. Mosley introduced Kelly to them as if they had known each other all their lives, not just the twelve hours on a train. They invited Kelly to go home with them.

"Just wait and take the next train tomorrow, Kelly," said Mr. Mosley. "You're welcome to stay at our home and get some rest before you continue on your journey."

"Thanks Mr. Mosley, I sure do appreciate the invitation, but I have a lot of railroad miles ahead of me. I'll just find me a cup of coffee in the depot here. I'll be catching 'Old # 97', and she should be arriving about six a.m. Much obliged for the offer though, I enjoyed your company," Kelly said as he shook Mr. Mosley hand. *Isn't that just like a Southerner?* he thought. *Tell a perfect stranger the most personal details of your life and then invite him home to spend the night.*

'Old # 97' was the main train that ran from New York City to New Orleans. She was supposed to arrive in Atlanta at six a.m. and depart at seven to continue on the down line. After leaving Atlanta, 'Old # 97' would head southwest towards Montgomery, Alabama. From Montgomery, it was a straight shot south to the town of Greenville, Alabama, and then southwest into New Orleans, Louisiana.

* * * * *

By nine a.m. that morning, Kelly was beginning to worry. 'Old # 97' had not arrived—bad weather up north, the station attendant reported.

"They're having a major snowstorm somewhere up in Pennsylvania, and the train is traveling mighty slowly. They've got workers out clearing the tracks, but it's slow going from what the telegraph message says. We'll have to sit tight; I'll give you updates as they are received. But right now, I have no idea when she'll be here."

Kelly was somewhat put out to say the least. He was tired and just wanted a place to lay his head. At least it was warm in the depot. By ten a.m., he decided to find himself a place to lie down. He picked a bench over against the far wall out of the way of the crowd and rummaged in his suitcase for something to use as a pillow. He pulled out two flannel shirts, balled them up to put under his head, and covered himself with his heavy coat. *Actually it is pretty comfortable,* he thought. *Or maybe I'm so worn out I could sleep most anywhere.* He figured if the train did arrive and he was asleep, there would be so much commotion he would wake up immediately.

When Kelly woke up, it was one p.m. He sat up, stretched, and dug in the suitcase in search of a comb for his hair. After he had repacked his shirts, he walked to the station attendant's desk at the far end of the station. "Is there any news on 'Old #97?" Kelly asked.

"Well, yes sir, received a telegraph message about an hour ago. She had just gotten into the Smokies and was about to stop in Ashville, N.C. Still has a lot of ice on her, I understand, but she don't foresee any more delays. Should be here at five p.m."

'Old # 97' finally pulled into the depot in Atlanta at five p.m., eleven hours behind schedule. That train was something to see. She was coated in ice; icicles hung down almost to the tracks underneath the train. The engineer and fireman stepped down from the train. Kelly thought at first they were black men; all that could be seen was the whites of their eyes. The coal dust had coated their faces and every visible inch of their person. The passengers who disembarked in Atlanta were a haggard looking lot too. The strain of the ordeal showed plainly on their faces and their clothes looked as if they had slept in them, which they had.

After an hour and half layover in Atlanta, 'Old #97' was ready to depart. The train crew had enough time to clean up a bit and get some hot food. "All aboard," shouted the conductor, "let's get this show on the road."

Kelly and all the other passengers boarded the train and she pulled out right at six thirty p.m., heading for Montgomery, Alabama. Kelly wouldn't be getting off in Montgomery; he was heading to Greenville, Alabama, to the south. Cyrus was meeting him there at the depot. *I guess Cyrus will be waiting a while. I sure hope he's long on patience,* Kelly thought.

The trip from Atlanta to Montgomery was pretty uneventful. There were no passengers like Mr. Mosley to entertain him, and traveling through the dark countryside, he had no scenery to captivate his mind. It had been interesting to Kelly to look at the land passing by the window, the houses, the fields, and the animals grazing the pasturelands. What were these people's lives like? Were they not the same as his family, eking out a living from the land and getting by the best they knew how? His imagination knew no bounds when he had the time to sit and ponder the scenes outside the train window.

Now with complete darkness covering the land—there were no electric lights in the Georgia and Alabama countryside—he could either let his mind dwell on his own feelings or try to get some sleep. He opted for the latter, crossed his arms, and leaned his head against the cold windowpane. He awakened with a start when the train came to a stop in Montgomery at one a.m. His mind had been lulled to unconsciousness with the rhythm of the rails beneath the train; that suddenly ceased and he sat bolt upright. The stop in Montgomery was for thirty minutes to take on water, mail, passengers and a coal tender. Kelly stood, stretched, and descended from the train. He stood there on the depot platform, enjoying the chill of the night air and the bustle of the crowd around him, just puffing on his pipe.

* * * * *

Cyrus was beginning to worry about his brother. He had waited in the depot at Greenville for almost four hours when the message came through that the train had been seriously delayed. By nine p.m., Cyrus made a decision. *I'll just go over to the Greenville Hotel and get us a room. By the time Kelly finally arrives, it will be far too late to travel tonight.*

Cyrus secured a room for him and Kelly at the hotel and then he returned to the depot to await his brother's arrival. At three thirty a.m., the train finally pulled into the station at Greenville. It was so late, there were few people waiting in the depot for the passengers, but Cyrus was there anxious to see his younger brother. When Kelly stepped down with his battered, old, brown suitcase, Cyrus hurried over to meet him.

"It's about time you got here, little brother. I heard the train was delayed up north so I got us a room for the night at the hotel; we'll start to Andalusia tomorrow. I knew you would be totally exhausted from the trip."

Kelly embraced Cyrus. "You're right, Brother. I sure am tired; I've been traveling almost thirty hours, including the time I sat in Atlanta. I know I look like hell. It will be so nice to just bathe and climb into a clean bed. Thanks for being so patient. I don't know what I would have done if I had arrived and you were not here. I would have been one ornery son of a bitch, I imagine."

* * * * *

At nine a.m. the following morning, Cyrus shook Kelly to wake him up. "I'm sorry to have to disturb your sleep, little brother, but we need to get us some breakfast and get on the road. It's a good seventy-five miles to the turpentine still from here, and I would like to get there and show you around before dark."

Kelly reluctantly climbed from his bed, washed his face, and dressed. They had breakfast at a little café right down from the hotel, checked out, and climbed into Cyrus's Model T automobile to finish the journey.

"This traveling sure takes it out of a man," Kelly said as they headed out of town.

It was a real pleasant trip. Kelly brought Cyrus up to date on all the folks at Rayflin and Cyrus told Kelly all about the turpentine business. At one p.m., they stopped in the little town of Georgianna, Alabama, for dinner, leaving there within an hour. They arrived at the turpentine still northwest of Andalusia before four in the afternoon.

"It's not much to see right now with the still sitting idle," Cyrus said. I just wanted to stop and speak to the fellows, let them know we're here."

Cyrus introduced Kelly to two white fellows, Holl Clayton and Lucian Andrews, who helped him run the operation. "I'll introduce you to some of my black workers tomorrow; they've already called it quits for today."

Kelly didn't get to look the still over; he would do that tomorrow and have Cyrus explain its operation. He had seen turpentine stills at work before but had not been interested in the process. Now that he would be working with Cyrus for the next three months, he intended to familiarize himself with how it worked. Kelly did notice the row of small shotgun houses two hundred yards away.

"That's where the black workers live," Cyrus said. "Tom Morris lives in the first house. He keeps watch on the property at night when we're gone; don't want any thieves stealing our equipment. He's a real dependable fellow; you'll like him." Turning towards his car, he said, "Come on, I'm anxious for you to see where I live. Let's go."

* * * * *

Cyrus's house was small, only four rooms, but comfortable about 5 miles away in the small community of River Falls. Holl and Lucian preferred to live in Andalusia, a bigger town with their families. Cyrus preferred small River Falls, so much like Steadman or even Rayflin, with only a country store at a crossroads and a few family homes.

That night, Cyrus told Kelly what he expected of him and talked more about the business.

"The turpentine business is a real lucrative venture right now, Kelly. Turpentine and rosin are used in the production of so many things. I'm not saying I'll get rich, but with all the pine forest the timber company owns in southern Alabama, my job is pretty secure. They pay me pretty well to manage the still for them and have even suggested they might consider sending me somewhere in north Florida to start an operation down there. I'm happy with what I'm doing. Besides, the land in southern Alabama looks just like home."

The next morning, bright and early, Kelly and Cyrus headed out to the turpentine still. The still itself wasn't running this time of year. It wouldn't start production again until spring, when the sap in the pines began to flow, but it was an impressive operation to Kelly.

There was a two-story covered shed about 20-foot by 40-foot, under which the actual turpentine still sat. This shed had a second floor, on which barrels sat at the front of the shed; the back half was open to accommodate the still and the smoke stack. There was a long platform nearby loaded with barrels to be filled with scraped gum and several storage sheds to accommodate the necessary tools for the process: boxing axes, hacks, pullers, scrapers, and buckets. There was also a small 16-foot by 12-foot building about 50 yards from the shed that was used as Cyrus's office.

"This is where you will be spending most of your time, Kelly," Cyrus said as he opened the door to the office. It was total disaster. There was a small desk with chair and a bookcase with ledgers and papers piled everywhere. "As you can see, it can use a little organization."

"I do believe you're right about that, Cyrus, it'll take me a month just to plow through all these papers," he declared, stepping inside and surveying the mayhem with a knowing gaze. "Then I'll have to set up a book-keeping process that makes sense to you. But then, that's what you hired me for."

Changing the subject, Cyrus said, "Come, let's walk over to the still and I'll give you a brief idea about how the thing works."

As they started across the yard between the office and the shed, Cyrus explained from the very beginning how the process worked.

"We begin with the collection of gun from the pine trees. A box is cut near the ground in the tree with a boxing axe. A tin box is attached to the deep cut at the base. The box will eventually hold up to a quart of pinesap. Streaks are cut into the pine above the box until the face of the tree is exposed about head high. This is what we turpentine men call a 'cat face.' A new streak has to be applied weekly during the summer and spring because the sap will dry out and get hard. When the sap is running, it drips down the side of the exposed tree surface and collects in the tin box. This is then dipped out into barrels to transport to the still. You got that so far, little brother?" Cyrus asked as he attempted to explain the whole process to Kelly.

"Hell, Cyrus, I know all about that part. Why, we've done that much on Pa's place at Rayflin. I just wanted you to tell me more about the still itself," Kelly replied.

"Ok, Kelly." By this time, they were standing underneath the shed beside the huge copper turpentine still. Cyrus began his explanation without hesitation; he knew the turpentine distillation business inside and out. "The main body of the still is this huge copper kettle; it will hold six barrels of gum at a time. The cap comes off the top and we pour in the gum; then the cap is put back on. This cap has a copper pipe, which is formed into a coil and runs through a tank of cool water. Once we get a good fire going under the still, we heat the gum to between three hundred and three hundred fifty degrees. As the gum boils steam and vapor forms and condenses into water and spirits of turpentine, this runs through the coiled copper pipe submerged in the tank of cool water. Both the turpentine and water run out of the coil into another barrel. Since the turpentine is much lighter, it flows off through a drainpipe at the top of the barrel and collects in a 50-gallon barrel; this is spirits of turpentine. What's left in the still after all the turpentine is distilled is called the rosin; it is drained off through a series of strainers to remove pieces of trash and dead insects and pours into a trough as clean rosin. It is then dipped into barrels and allowed to cool and harden. The barrels of rosin and pure turpentine are then ready to be shipped. That pretty much sums up the process. But it is important to know what the hell you are doing because you don't want to over or under heat the gum; it won't be as good a quality. The distilling process also creates gases that are extremely flammable and could explode under the right conditions. That's why I have to keep a close watch on the still when she is all fired up."

"Well, Cyrus, sounds like you know your business; now I have a good idea of how she works. But since my place is in your office over yonder, I guess I'll get over there and get started on those books."

Twenty

A GUST OF COLD WIND OUT OF THE NORTH BLEW THE DRIED walnut leaves around Mary's feet, whipping her long skirt against her legs as she bent over to gather firewood. The wood piles thirty feet to the right of the front porch were still high. Kelly had made sure Mary had plenty of firewood before he left. He had segregated the wood into two piles: dried pine for low fires to get them going and green oak and hickory that burned longer so they would last. With all this wood Kelly had cut, Mary and Sibbie wouldn't have to worry about fuel to keep the house warm. He had also cut a good supply of 'fat lighter' that was beginning to dwindle. The 'fat lighter' was used whenever a fire had to be started from scratch. A few pieces of fat pine splinters and a match were all that were necessary.

Sibbie or me will have to take a croaker sack and an ax to the woods soon and cut some splinters from those old pine stumps, Mary thought. She held an armload of green wood, bent her head against the wind, and hurried to the front porch to deposit her burden into the wood box. It sat outside by the kitchen door within easy reach for the fireplace and Mary's wood cook stove.

It will be dark soon, Mary thought. *We have to get those children fed and in the bed.* After three more trips to the woodpile, the box was filled to the top and Mary, carrying three pieces of green hickory, opened the kitchen door and went in. A gust of cold air followed her inside as she turned to shut the door, caused her skirt to billow and the flames in the fireplace to flicker brightly.

"Lordy, Miss Mary, it must really be getting cold outside. That howling wind sounds just like the 'haints' my granny Chaney is always telling us children about."

"Surely, Sibbie, you don't believe in ghosts?" Mary asked with lifted brows, adding the hickory logs to the fire. A shower of sparks flew up the chimney and a loud popping noise resounded from the fire.

"Well, no, Miss Mary, I guess I don't really, but my granny sure does, and I ain't one to be disbelieving. Just because I haven't had the misfortune to see one, don't mean they ain't real."

Sibbie stood at the wood cook stove with her back to Mary, cooking the children some gruel for their supper. The day before, Sibbie had killed a chicken, plucked the feathers off, gutted, and cleaned it. They had chicken and dumplings for dinner and supper yesterday and now the remainder of the chicken broth was beginning to boil on the stovetop. She added cornmeal; when it thickened, it became gruel for their supper.

The children were in the next room. A potbellied wood heater was in this room and a small fire was kept burning in it for the children's comfort. This was a better place for the children to play when they were inside, with no open fireplace and within earshot of the women working in the kitchen. Leon and Louise were playing with their baby sister. She was eight months old now, could sit up, and was just beginning to crawl.

Just beginning to get interesting, Leon thought. He picked Elsie up from the floor and sat her inside a cardboard box; both Leon and Louise were making faces at her just to hear her squeal with laughter.

"Come on, children, your supper is on the table," Mary said as she bent down and scooped Elsie from the box. "And you're having some gruel too, little girl, then a bottle, a diaper change, and the bed, in that order."

After the children had their fill of the chicken gruel, they were bathed in front of the fire and dressed for bed. Mary had buried two bricks in the coals underneath the fire earlier. She fished these out with the fire poker, picked them up gingerly with potholders, and wrapped them in towels to place in Leon and Louise's bed to give their little bodies a head start in warming the cold covers.

While Sibbie stayed with Leon and Louise in the kitchen, Mary opened the kitchen door, carrying a sleeping Elsie, wrapped in a blanket against the cold. There was a stiff breeze blowing and Mary heard the creaking of the chains that suspended the swing at far end of the porch. She opened the hall door to access the bedrooms from the front porch; the wind closed the outside door behind her.

A kerosene lamp burned on the side table in the hallway. Sibbie could always be depended on to light the lamp as soon as the sun set so they could find their way to bed in the dark. Mary tucked Elsie into her bed with the straight back of a chair pushed against the side so she wouldn't tumble off, covering her with a thick quilt. Mary had hung Elsie's blanket in front of the fire to warm it before swaddling Elsie inside. Her own body heat inside the warmed blanket would assure her comfort until her mother joined her later in the double bed.

When Elsie was all settled, Mary returned to the kitchen for the other two while Sibbie washed the supper dishes. As soon as Louise and Leon were tucked into their beds with several quilts over them and warm bricks at their feet, Mary returned again to the kitchen to spend some time conversing with Sibbie.

It had become an evening ritual for Mary and Sibbie to sit in front of the fireplace in the kitchen for a couple of hours after the children were tucked in. They would sit in front of the fire, waiting for it to die down, and talk for a while. There were usually newspapers Mary had brought home from Rayflin when she took the children to visit their grandparents on Sunday afternoons. These she would read to Sibbie and they would discuss the articles. Kelly had been gone a little over a month now and he had written to Mary twice. These letters she reread to herself most every night before turning in for the evening. When they were first received, she had shared parts of them with Sibbie.

"I know it's seems silly to reread these letters every night. I should have them memorized by now."

"No, Miss Mary I don't think it silly at all," Sibbie replied. "I know you miss Mr. Kelly and reading his words reminds you of him. If I had a man way out in Alabama and he wrote me such nice letters, I would reread them too every chance I got, that is, if I could read."

"You know, Sibbie, that would be a good way for us to pass the time together in the evenings. I'll teach you your letters and how to read. I'm not a teacher, but I will be glad to give it a try."

"Oh, Miss Mary!" Sibbie said, excitement sounding in her voice. "It would be wonderful if you could teach me to read! I would be forever grateful."

"It's settled then, Sibbie. From now on, while you're staying here, we'll have a lesson after the children are in bed."

* * * * *

Sitting in front of the fire in those dark, still evenings waiting for it to burn down to embers, Mary and Sibbie became good friends. They respected each other. Sibbie respected Mary because she was a kind, hardworking lady who loved her children devotedly, but at the same time made them behave themselves. Mary respected Sibbie because even though she was just a young girl of fourteen, she was dependable, a hard worker, and patient with the children. Besides, Sibbie was good company. It was hard with Kelly away and all the chores Mary's sole responsibility. Mary cooked, cleaned, carried wood, and tended to the animals and children with Sibbie's help.

Through the cold, black nights of February, they sat together with paper spread on the table beneath the kerosene lamp. The only noises were the crackling fire at their back and the howl of the wind whipping around the corners of the house; sometimes there was the occasional yelp of a fox below the spring. Mary taught Sibbie how to read and write beside the kitchen fire. First, she taught her the alphabet and how to write the letters. Sibbie practiced her letters every evening until she could recite them by heart.

"I am so proud of myself, Miss Mary. I didn't ever think I would learn my letters. Ma and Pa will be so surprised." She was such an eager student that some nights they stayed up way longer than they should, absorbed in their task.

"I'm proud of you too, Sibbie, but this is just the beginning. Now you're going to learn the sounds that each letter makes and then we will progress to short words. You'll be reading before you know it."

* * * * *

By early March, Mary's daffodils were peeping up through the ground. The worst of the cold weather had passed, even though quilts were still necessary on their beds; warming bricks were not. Sibbie slept in the room with Louise on a small cot. Sometimes during the night when she awoke, she would check on Louise and tiptoe across the hall to Leon's bed just to make sure he wasn't out from under his covers. She didn't worry about Elsie; she knew Mary kept her covered during the night.

Spring seemed to be in the air. When they awoke in the mornings before good daylight, the birds could be heard twittering to each other in the magnolia by the back steps. The hyacinths and crocus bulbs Mary had planted last fall around the walnut tree in the backyard burst through the ground in a profusion of pinks, blues, and purples. Whenever Leon and Louise played outside in the pleasant days of March, they were sorely tempted to pick their momma's flowers but knew better. Mary gave them permission to cut a bouquet with Sibbie's supervision.

"My, don't our flowers look pretty," Louise said to Leon. Louise was so proud of their flowers, which were stuck in a quart fruit jar half full of water in the middle of the kitchen table.

"They're a bunch of pretty flowers in a fruit jar, Louise, don't go on so," Leon replied.

"They're not just that, silly boy," Louise said proudly. "They're also what ladies would call decoration to brighten a drab table."

"Ok, children, enough discussion about the bouquet of flowers," Mary interrupted. "They are pretty and Louise is right; they do brighten the table."

* * * * *

It was almost planting time; Mary didn't know a whole lot about plowing the fields. She could hitch the mule to the plow with no trouble, but had never attempted to plow straight furrows in a ten-acre field. She had no need to worry herself; Joe and Ab Hardy and Arthur Moore showed up early the morning of March 18th and took charge of planting Kelly's fields.

"Thank you, boys, so much for taking care of the planting for me," Mary said when they stopped by that afternoon to let her know what they had done and what they intended.

"You're mighty welcome, Miss Mary," Ab said. "We just expect to help plant these fields for Mr. Kelly and since he's way off in Alabama and it's getting to be planting time, we decided to get started."

Twenty-One

IT WAS SOON APRIL. KELLY HAD BEEN IN ALABAMA ALMOST three months and Mary was ready for him to get back home. He had written her long letters about twice a month, explaining Cyrus's operation and what a time he was having trying to organize his books. *I should be home by April fifteenth if all goes as planned,* Kelly wrote. *I sure will be happy to see all of you.*

"Only two more weeks, Sibbie; Kelly should be home and I can rest easy," Mary said as they sat at the kitchen table one evening over Sibbie's lessons. "And don't you worry; I will be more than happy to continue helping you with reading. You can come up here in the afternoons before supper. Leon and Louise are old enough to keep an eye on the baby for me for an hour or so if we're close by."

"I would like that, Miss Mary. I have missed being at home with my folks, but I have enjoyed staying here with you and the children. I've saved all the money you paid me and I'm going to keep that tucked away for safe-keeping until a 'rainy day' when me or my folks need it."

Mary received a postcard from Kelly on the twelfth of April. "Cyrus is taking me to Greenville, Alabama, on the fifteenth to catch the train home, Kelly wrote. I should be in Rayflin the afternoon of the sixteenth. If you and the children could be at Ma and Pa's when I step down from that train, I would sure be a happy man."

Mary was so excited for the next four days; she could hardly contain her enthusiasm. The children couldn't help but notice how happy their mother was.

"Momma, you hum to yourself all the time," Leon observed. "And why are you smiling all the time?"

"Well, Son, your daddy is coming home in a few days. We're all going down to Rayflin to meet him when he steps off the train."

"I sure will be glad when my daddy gets home too," Leon said. "I'm tired of living with nothing but a bunch of girls."

At nine o'clock in the morning on the sixteenth of April, Mary had all the children clean, dressed, and ready to head to Rayflin. She didn't expect Kelly until the evening train passed through around 2:00 p.m., but she figured his parents would be more than happy to see the children. What if he was on the morning train from Batesburg? She didn't want to risk him arriving and them not being there to greet him. Sibbie had hitched the mule to the buggy for her and helped get the children aboard. Sibbie climbed in the back with her old straw suitcase beside her; she was going back home and Mary would drop her by on the way.

"No sense in you walking, Sibbie, we'll be passing right by your house."

Peninnah and Kel were so glad to see their grandchildren when Mary pulled the buggy in beside the house at Rayflin.

"So Kelly will be getting home today," Mr. Kel said. "I'll be right glad to see the boy myself; seems like he has been gone a year, not just three months. I know his brothers have missed him, and Roston has been complaining about running that store without Kelly here to back him up." Mr. Kel seemed to drone on and on to Mary. "Kelly's the manager; Roston's more into entertaining the customers rather than making money. I guess with Kelly back, Roston can do some serious courting; found him a right sweet little girl lives over near the chalk mine, Farrie Jeffcoat. I think she might be the one to settle that boy down. I'm hoping so anyways." Mr. Kel paused.

Finally Mary could reply. "It does seem like a long time since he left. I know he has missed us all and helping Roston run the store. He'll be glad to get back to it I'm sure."

* * * * *

They had dinner at noon and time seemed to drag. The Swamp Rabbit would pass through around two p.m. from Batesburg heading to Perry, and Mary was beside herself anticipating Kelly arriving on that two o'clock train. Mary, Miss Penninah, and the children sat on the front porch, waiting to hear the train whistle; hopefully Kelly would be on it.

A squirrel entertained the children from the big magnolia that shadowed the porch; he chattered and waved his bushy tail from his perch above the porch roof. They all laughed as the little squirrel jumped from one branch to another above their heads.

Leon suggested, "If only I had a slingshot, we could be having squirrel for supper."

"You wouldn't dare kill that little squirrel! Louise exclaimed. "That would be so mean."

"It wouldn't be mean if we had him for supper," Leon replied. "Girls are so silly, it's just a little ole squirrel."

"Is not," Louise said. "It one of God's creatures, just like you."

"Is to, just a squirrel."

"Hush, children, right this minute. I'm already nervous with anticipation, I don't intend to listen to any more bickering from you two," Mary said as she gave them that look they knew so well. Louise and Leon both understood and knew to straighten up or there would be trouble. No more was said about the little bushy-tailed squirrel.

* * * * *

At precisely 10 minutes past two, the train whistle blasted as the Swamp Rabbit's engine came within sight of Rayflin, a signal that passengers or mail was to be dropped off here.

"It's Daddy! It's Daddy!" Louise and Leon squealed as they jumped down the front steps.

"Louise and Leon, you two stop right there. We have to wait for the train to stop. Get yourselves back up on the porch this minute," Mary commanded.

They both reluctantly climbed back up the steps as they were told. Mr. Kel heard the whistle from up at the barn and headed towards the tracks.

The Swamp Rabbit came to a screeching halt in front of the passenger shack; smoke boiling from the stack.

Kelly stepped from the train, his clothes wrinkled and thick stubble on his face. But the thing Mary noticed the most was the wide grin that spread across his face and the twinkle in his eyes as they alighted on his two children running from the house to greet him. He swooped Leon and Louise up in his arms and gave them both a big kiss as Mary, who was holding Elsie, Kel, and Peninnah walked up. He put the children down and hugged Mary and the baby.

"It's so good to see you, Mary, and how my little Elsie has grown."

"I'm so glad you are finally here, Kelly, we missed you so," Mary said as she rested her hand on his shoulder.

"And you have no idea how much I have missed all of you," he said grinning from ear to ear. He greeted his ma with a hug and his pa with a handshake.

"We're all glad you're back, boy," Mr. Kel said. "I know you'll be wanting to get on to your house this afternoon, but me and your ma will look forward to you telling us all about the trip and how Cyrus is getting along, maybe over dinner Sunday."

"That's a deal, Pa. I'll tell y'all all the details then, but I'm sure I'll be back down here sometime tomorrow to see how Roston is doing in the store. Mary wrote that the fellows were planting my fields. I've got to see how that's coming along—all the seeds should be in the ground by now," Kelly said.

Kelly didn't even go inside his parent's house. He was anxious to get home, and so was Mary. She was so relieved to have him home again. Kelly boosted the children into the buggy, climbed in beside Mary, lifted the reins, and with a slap across the mule's back, they were on their way home.

* * * * *

While Mary fixed them some supper, Kelly took a quick walk through his fields.

"Those boys have really done a good job it looks like to me. The corn is already up a few inches and the wheat and oats are sprouting," Kelly commented at the supper table.

When the meal was done, he spent some time playing with the children and answering Louise and Leon's questions while Mary fixed the cot in Louise's room for Elsie and got her to sleep. Kelly carried the other two to their beds and tucked them in.

"It is such a nice evening, Kelly, let's sit for a little while on the front porch and talk."

He told Mary all about Alabama, the things he saw and the people he met. "And Mary, I have close to $400.00 cash money in my suitcase. I'll have to think long and hard before I spend any of that."

They rocked gently in the porch rockers, listening to the crickets chirping and watching the pinpoint lights of the lightening bugs across the road in the woods. The only light was from the heaven of stars above and the dim light of the kerosene lamp in the hallway shining through the open door. The air was warm, but a breeze stirred the new leaves on the walnut tree in their yard; the tops of the pines and oaks in the dark woods swayed ever so slightly against the backdrop of the night sky.

"The moon will be up soon, Mary, let's get to bed. It sure has been lonesome sleeping on that cot at Cyrus's with no one to snuggle up to but his old dog, Snow."

* * * * *

That was the spring that Kelly's sister, Jennie, married Olin Rish. It was in April of 1916, barely two weeks after Kelly came home, when she and Olin tied the knot. Olin was a distant cousin of Jennie's. His mother, Miss Clementine, had been a Gantt herself before she married Olin's father, George Rish. Olin was a tall, slender fellow, over 6 feet tall, with dark skin inherited from some Indian forbearer. Kel didn't call Olin by his Christian name; it was always Rish. Soon after their marriage, Olin and Jennie moved into a small four-room house off the main road down on Pelt Branch and set up housekeeping. Jennie's brothers, Roston, Woodard, and Sam, had helped Olin with the construction so it would be ready when the big day came.

Kelly soon developed a cautious demeanor towards Olin Rish; he felt Olin was untrustworthy, and Kelly was normally good at first impressions. Roston, Woodard, and Sam had helped Olin build the house on Pelt Branch and Sam told Kelly, "Something just doesn't sit right as far as Olin's personality." They got along with him well enough, but he seemed to be devious from what they could surmise from the stories he told and the comments he made about people he had dealt with in the past.

"I'll venture this much about Olin Rish," Sam told Kelly, "the jury is still out on whether Jennie made a good choice in Rish, as Pa calls him."

Now, three of Kel and Peninnah's children, Kelly, Corrie, and Jennie, were married. Roston and Woodard had good prospects. Roston had started courting Farrie Jeffcoat. Woodard was courting

Mamie Hall, Mr. Willie Hall's daughter from up at Steadman. Sam, Rion, and Buck were still footloose and fancy free as far as women were concerned. Every weekend, they were courting, drinking, and playing cards.

To Mary's dismay, after Kelly returned from Alabama, he spent a good deal of his time with his brothers drinking. He didn't drink during the week when there was work to be done on the farm, but in the evenings, especially on Saturday nights when the work week was behind him, he and the boys usually 'tied one on.'

Twenty-Two

IN OCTOBER OF 1916, LEON BEGAN HIS SCHOOLING AT A one-room school at the head of Mr. Abe Hall's pond in Steadman, barely two hundred yards southeast of the train depot. Miss Opie Barr, a spinster woman from over near Samaria, taught forty-five pupils ranging in age from six to sixteen from the surrounding community.

School started for the community children that month and ran through July, planned that way so it didn't interfere with the busiest time of harvesting the crops. So many of the older children were needed to help on the farm; it made no sense for school to be in session when half the children could not attend. Very few students continued their education past the age of sixteen; in an agrarian society, book learning was not a high priority. "It's important to learn to read and write, and to have simple math skills," farmers agreed amongst themselves, "but higher education is not in great demand in the backcountry of South Carolina. What need do farmers and sawmill workers have to be formally educated?"

Kelly took Leon to school his first day and signed him in. After that, Leon walked from their house up the road a half mile to Uncle Jule and Aunt Corrie's place, where cousin Nina Lee joined him.

They both followed the railroad tracks into Steadman to school. Mary was worried about her young son walking all that way and then having to contend with older children at school. She was afraid the older boys would pick on Leon the way children sometimes do. She didn't need to worry; even at the age of six, Leon could pretty much hold his own. He was fearless, full of confidence in himself, and ready to fight at the drop of a hat if necessary. Those older boys didn't intimidate him at all.

School had barely been in session a month the first time Leon got in trouble. He had arrived at school with a big wad of chewing gum in his mouth. Actually, he was pretending it was tobacco. He had a good size chew when Miss Barr noticed. There was already a nip to the air; that morning, some of the older boys had built a fire in their potbellied stove in the center of the schoolroom.

Well, when Miss Barr noticed Leon chewing, she said, "Leon Gantt, drop that gum in the stove this instant." Leon was not defiant. He knew grown-ups were to be obeyed; his momma had taught him that much. He got up from his desk, slid the stove eye from the top with the iron-stove lever and dropped the gum in. Of course, by the time he was seated at his desk, another slab of gum had been inserted in his mouth. Miss Barr noticed right away that the offending gum was still there. Again, she told him to drop the gum in the top of the stove.

"This time, Leon, hold that gum up so I can see you drop it in."

Leon obliged but he had more tucked in the pocket of his dungarees. At first Miss Barr tried to ignore the breach in behavior, knowing the other children would only be entertained if she persisted with making him spit the gum in the stove. Pretty soon, she could stand the giggles and smacking no longer.

"Leon, would you please come to the front of the class." Leon obeyed and stood before Miss Barr, thinking he might have pushed the little joke too far. Miss Barr held out the palm of her hand. "Leon please spit your gum in here and turn those dungaree pockets inside out." Well, Leon did as he was told; he spit the gum into her outstretched palm and turned his pockets out. The gum fell to the floor, along with a little garter snake he had picked up on the way to school that morning. The snake had been cold and unmoving when Leon had spotted it by the road this morning. He had thought it was dead, intending to carry it home to terrify Louise. Evidently the November temperatures had something to do with its comatose state. In Leon's pocket, it had warmed up and as soon as it hit the floor, it began to wiggle away. All the children leaped from their desks; the girls squealed and climbed in their chairs while the boys laughed hysterically. Miss Barr did not think it funny at all. She was a bit shocked, even let out a little squeal, but soon composed herself. It was only a little garter snake and nothing to get excited about.

"I'm sorry about that, Miss Barr!" Leon yelled over the din of laugher, scrambling to recover the little snake.

"Take that thing outside and let it go right this minute before everyone gets out of hand," Miss Barr answered in a not-so-pleasant, high-toned voice. With emphasis, she said, "Do not *ever* bring another snake into my classroom, is that understood? I'm sure your mother, Mrs. Gantt, would be interested in your behavior and could probably get the message across better than I."

"Yes, Ma'am," is all Leon could reply. He figured Cousin Nina Lee would blab her mouth to Aunt Corrie and his momma would surely find out. He could just imagine her reaction. The class simmered down after the snake was banished to the yard. Leon became a model student the rest of the day, quiet, mannerly, and docile. He was so nice, Miss Barr talked herself out of reporting his behavior to his momma, but she did warn him after school.

"Your bad behavior will not be tolerated. Any repeat will require swift retribution; next time, you will be paddled soundly on your posterior." Of course, Leon had no clue what a posterior was, but he got the general idea.

Leon became the perfect student for Miss Barr because he knew she would not tolerate any misbehaving on his part. He could have been in deep trouble with his momma if she had told about the snake incident, but she had not. He developed a kinship with Miss Barr, knowing he deserved a sound switching but had gotten by on her good graces. Nina Lee didn't tell either; she had no desire to get Leon in trouble, and besides, she knew if the tables had been turned, he would have kept silent about her misbehavior.

* * * * *

By the end of November, Leon had to wear shoes to school. He was used to going barefoot and hated the new leather lace-up brogans Kelly had ordered for him from the Sears and Roebuck catalog.

Every morning, Mary woke Leon, saying with a gentle shake, "It's 6:00 in the morning, Leon, get up and get ready for school. I've got your breakfast on the stove." He never had to be called twice. First of all, he looked forward to school, and secondly, he knew his momma meant what she said and it wouldn't end well if she had to call him a second time. He grabbed his clothes from the chair in his room, put his socks on and dashed across the porch to the kitchen. His getting dressed in front of the kitchen fire felt a lot better than in his bedroom in the winter time. After eating his breakfast of grits, butter, and sometimes fried fatback, he hurried out the door.

Nina Lee was always waiting on the porch at Aunt Corrie and Uncle Jule's for her cousin to come sailing down the road. He ran most of the way, at least to Nina Lee's. In the winter, the cold didn't seem nearly as bad if you ran. As soon as Nina Lee joined him, he slowed his pace so they could talk. During the winter months, they didn't dilly-dally too much; the temperature urged them to get indoors beside a stove. The warmer the days got, the slower the two got on the walk to school. By spring, they were awfully close to being tardy. It was hard for two six-year-olds to ignore the wildflowers beside the road, the buzzing insects flitting around them, and little animals scurrying through the woods and fields they passed. Lizards, frogs, and snakes that had the misfortune to cross Leon's path were always ending up in his pockets. These he was certain to remove before he crossed the threshold of Miss Barr's class. There was an old bucket once used at the well propped against the outside wall of the school, no longer any good because it had small cracks in the bottom. He always deposited any critters he had collected beside the wall and turned the bucket over them, to be picked up on the way home. They would survive due to the less than airtight environment under the bucket.

* * * * *

The War still raged in Europe, but the United States was not in the fight. At least no American soldiers had been sent halfway around the world to fight in those foreign lands. Whenever Miss Barr had a history lesson for the older children, they always talked about the War in Europe. The younger children were not expected to participate; they were supposed to be practicing their letters or sums, but Leon always paid attention when the War was being discussed. *My daddy or some of my uncles could end up in that War yet*, Leon surmised. *Best to listen to Miss Barr and know what the score is.*

On February 1, 1917, Germany again changed their policy to unrestricted submarine warfare on all shipping. Leon did not understand exactly what this meant.

The way Miss Barr put it, "Those blasted Germans are sinking all ships, no matter their mission or the nationality of those on board. In an effort to end the War, Germany is attacking all American shipments of armaments and food to Great Britain and Europe." Leon might not understand, but he knew it was serious.

On February 17, 1917, the Cunard passenger liner Laconia set sail from New York to England; a man who worked for the Chicago Tribune was on board when she was sunk by the German U boats. The newspaperman survived the sinking and wrote a terrifying description of the event that was published in his paper. The article published in the Tribune supposedly had a lot to do with the United States changing her policy of not to get involved. The article was also published in almost all major newspapers in the country and Miss Barr shared it with her older students during their history lesson.

Miss Barr said, "I fear this is the straw that broke the camel's back." Two months later, in April 1917, the United States would declare war on Germany.

Twenty-Three

IT WAS HARD FOR MARY TO HANG THE WASH; THE MARCH wind blew so ferociously, the garments slipped from her fingers and whipped around the clothesline. The children, playing a game of marbles between the chinaberry trees in the backyard, were buffeted by the wind. Sand accumulated in their clothing and hair. At times, the wind was so strong, they huddled together against the trunk of the giant chinaberry. Just as the wind seemed to die down a bit so they could continue their game, a gust would descend from above and interrupt their play. It was hard enough keeping Elsie from removing their marbles from the circle drawn on the ground, but to contend with the blowing sand *and* Elsie was too much.

"Come, children, let's get inside," called Mary. Your dinner is ready and this wind is blowing too hard for you three to play outside."

They ran up the back steps into the dining room, shaking sand from their clothes as they entered the back door. "My, what a mess on my floor. Louise, get the broom and sweep for me please. It's so windy y'all will have to play inside this afternoon." It was Saturday, so there was no school.

* * * * *

Kelly was at the chalk mine; he and Roston had both accepted jobs there the first of the year. Roston was acting superintendent and Kelly was his foreman. The pay was good; Kelly made $1.50 a day working five days, eight a.m. to six p.m., and seventy-five cents for the five hours he worked on Saturday. Roston, as superintendent, made almost twice as much. Roston still ran the store at Rayflin in the evenings and on Saturday afternoons. Kelly helped out in the store and managed his farming on the side. He had Ab, Joe, and Arthur planting his fields for him, so he didn't worry about the crops. They were all dependable. Good farmers themselves, he only needed to oversee their progress.

* * * * *

As soon as the children had their dinner, Leon said, "Momma, would it be all right if we play outside in the old kitchen house? It's empty and we will have lots of room to roll our marbles. You said yourself, it's too windy for us to play in the yard."

"Yes, you can, but take the baby with you and watch her. I have to get these dishes cleaned up."

The three headed down the back steps towards the kitchen house. Leon had his bag of marbles they could roll across the floor. Louise carried a top to spin, and Elsie had her baby doll. The wind still howled, whipping Louise and Elsie's dresses around their legs as they walked. The children stepped up onto the small porch and Leon undid the door latch. It was dark inside until Leon opened the two shuttered windows to let in enough light for them to play.

There was a lingering smell of charred hickory in the air from the old fireplace; the eight-inch wide floorboards were smooth from the tread of feet over the many years it had previously been in use. Now Mary used it for storage and kept her canned jams, jellies, and vegetables on shelves Kelly had built on one wall.

Over to the right was a #3 washtub full of ashes. Mary dumped the ashes left from their fires here, saving them to put around her peanuts. This added potash to the soil. There were also three forty-eight pound kegs of lard.

Leon and Louise immediately squatted on the floor and begin to roll marbles to the back of the kitchen house. They weren't watching Elsie as she wandered over to a keg of lard and managed to lift the lid. Dipping her hands into the white slick lard, Elsie begins to stir. That's when she got the idea to add ashes to the mixture. Leon and Louise were oblivious to Elsie's actions; they were too engrossed in their game of marbles.

When Mary opened the kitchen house door to check on the children, what she found was absolutely astonishing and very upsetting. While Leon and Louise were busy at play, they had ignored two-year-old Elsie, definitely not watching her as instructed. Elsie had ashes well mixed into the keg of lard and was up to her elbows in the mixture.

"What have you two let the baby get into?" Mary exclaimed in dismay.

Leon and Louise realized too late that Elsie had stirred up a mess. Louise was the closest, so Mary grabbed her first and tore up her little behind good. Leon ran past his momma, crawled up under the house, and huddled by the kitchen chimney. He knew just as soon as his momma got hold of him, he would get the same as Louise. Mary led a crying Louise and a greasy, gray Elsie from the kitchen house. She would deal with Leon later; right now, she had to get Elsie cleaned up.

Leon huddled underneath the house beside the chimney the rest of the afternoon. Mary had squatted down once beside the back steps and told him to come out from under there. Normally he would have immediately obeyed his momma, but he knew he was going to get a whipping either way, so he might as well delay it as long as possible. About sundown, Kelly came home. He had worked at the chalk mine then remained at Rayflin helping Roston at the store.

"Where is Leon?" Kelly asked as they sat down at the supper table.

Mary told him the whole story. She began with the windy conditions, permission to play in the old kitchen house, and the results of Elsie's close proximity to the lard and ashes unsupervised. "Louise has already received her punishment for not watching the baby like she was told to do. That trifling son of yours is still under the house and won't come out."

After supper, Kelly went out the back door and squatted beside the steps. "Son, it's almost night, you need to come out from under this house. It's going to be awfully dark next to that chimney pretty soon."

"Daddy, you know if I come out from under this house, I'll feel like I'm in a hornet's nest when Momma gets a hold on me."

"I tell you what, Son, just this once, I'll tell your Momma to let you by with a warning. After all, you have been squatting beside that chimney for the last four hours. That's pretty bad punishment in itself I think. Now come on out."

Leon reluctantly crawled out from under the house. When he stood up, his body ached all over from the cramped position he had endured so long; he had spider webs in his hair and he was filthy from wallowing in the dry, black dirt under the house. True to his word, Kelly persuaded Mary to forego the whipping. "I think he has punished his own self this time," Kelly added.

Mary agreed Leon had been punished enough. "Leon," she told her son after supper was finished, "just this once, I agree with your daddy. You have been sufficiently punished by spending all that time squatting beside the chimney under the house." Continuing, she cautioned him that she would not accept any more excuses for disobedience. "When I tell you to tend to your baby sister, I expect you to keep an eye on her. This time there will be no spanking, but remember what I am saying and pay attention to your duty as the eldest next time. I have to be able to depend on you, Son, don't forget that."

"I won't forget, Mamma, honest injun," Leon replied. When Mary walked away, he let out a big audible sigh of relief as a smile crossed his face.

Twenty-Four

IN JUNE 1917, THE FIRST AMERICAN SOLDIERS WERE SENT TO France to fight the Germans in the trenches. All of America was geared up for the war effort to support the troops. This was all bewildering to Leon, but he did listen as his parents discussed the War around the supper table in the evenings or read articles from the newspapers.

In the mist of all the war fever, Roston, at the ripe old age of thirty-nine, married Miss Farrie Fable Jeffcoat on August 20 of '17.

All Mr. Kel could say was, "It's about time that boy settled down and raised a family. I didn't think I would live long enough to see any of Roston's children, but I might after all." Roston and Farrie moved into Roston's house at Rayflin and soon Farrie was expecting their first child.

"You know, Mary, I have to go register at the draft board," Kelly stated solemnly one night in September while they were discussing the War.

"Surely, Kelly, you won't have to go. You're not a young man. Besides, farming is so important to the war effort—that should make you exempt. You also have three young children."

"You're probably right, Mary. The government wants us to produce all the crops we can, especially the food crops. Cotton is important too, with all the cloth needed for uniforms and such for the soldiers. But I have to go and do my patriotic duty nonetheless. Woodard, Sam, Roston and I will be going to Lexington in a day or two to register."

That was in September of 1917. The next month in October, school at Steadman started again, this time Louise would accompany Leon and Nina Lee on the trek each morning. Leon had to slow his pace from home to Nina Lee's; Louise was just a girl and couldn't keep up.

* * * * *

In early December of '17, Kelly, Rion, Buck, and Olin were in the process of making some Christmas liquor. Sam found out about it; at that time, he was serving as a deputy sheriff for the county. In that capacity, he felt it was his duty to at least let his pa Kel know about the still. He knew Kel would take care of it once he knew them boys had a still on his place at Rattlesnake Branch.

After breakfast, Kel said, "Niney, I have somewhere to go," got up from the table, went out to the shed, got his axe on his shoulder, and headed into the swamp; he never said a word to the boys as to where he was headed. He found the still just where Sam had told him it would be and busted all the barrels with his axe. Kel picked up the still, took it deeper into the swamp, and threw it into some Gall Berry bushes.

Returning to Rayflin, he addressed Kelly, who was sitting on the porch. "Kelly."

"What you want, Pa?"

"If you want your hog scalding barrel, it's up there in the swamp, beat all to hell."

"Pa, you didn't beat my hog scalding barrel all to pieces, mine is up at the house."

"Well, whose barrel was it?" Kel asked.

"If you beat any Pa," Kelly replied, "it belonged to Olin, not me."

"Well, Rish told me he didn't have anything to do with that business on Rattlesnake Branch. Damn his time, he told me a flat-out lie."

"Well, Pa, I thought you knew by now Olin isn't a hundred per-cent honest when it comes to saving his own hide; remember that next time where Olin is concerned."

* * * * *

When the weather turned cold that winter, they had another threat to contend with. In December of '17 and into the winter months of January and February 1918, the whole country was in the throes of a flu pandemic.

It was so widespread and devastating that the President of the United States, Woodrow Wilson said in his address, "All Americans will you please discontinue public meetings and stay in your homes? That is the only way to stem the tide of the spreading flu pandemic."

Church services were discontinued and those in the community that died from the influenza were only accorded a graveside service. The congregation did not allow the bodies of the deceased to be laid out in the sanctuary for fear of contamination. This caused hard feelings towards the church for years to come by many of the grieving families. School was even closed in January and February of that year for fear the flu would spread.

None of the Gantt boys went to war and all the family survived the pandemic.

Their profession, farming, was too important to require they leave the home front to fight overseas. As far as not contracting the flu, Sam had a theory about that. "I believe it's the alcohol, boys, it kills all them flu germs."

* * * * *

By the time summer arrived in earnest that year of 1918, two more of Kel and Peninnah's children had married. Cyrus married Beulah Vann in February somewhere in north Florida, and Woodard married Mamie Hall in Steadman. He and Mamie were living in a small, two-room house in Steadman until they could have their own built. Woodard was planning to open a store of his own in Steadman with the help and advice of his father in law, Willie Hall. There were already four stores in Steadman run by Willie Hall, Boyd Hall, Thomas Quattlebaun, and Ed Gunter. Woodard's would make five. Steadman was a busy little place, not quite considered a town by the inhabitants because of the rural flavor. It was town nevertheless, with a post office, train depot, school, cotton gin, and mercantile establishments where most anything could be purchased, from a suit of clothes to a ton of brick.

* * * * *

In the fall of '18, Kelly, with the help of his brother, Sam, tore down the old kitchen house. They no longer needed the building, since the kitchen was now part of the main house. Besides, it took up a lot of space in the back yard. Space Leon, Louise, and Elsie could have for play. Mary could add to her growing flowers. She seemed to love digging in the dirt as much as her children. She had put in a pecan tree and a magnolia the winter before; they both were growing well. Mary absolutely had a green thumb, something not everyone was blessed with.

"Kelly, why don't we use the lumber from this old kitchen building to build a smokehouse at the edge of the backyard?" Sam asked.

"That's a good idea, Sam; it might be nice at that to have a smokehouse. I have eight or ten pigs that are right good size; we could butcher a couple of them come cold weather and use the smoke house to cure the bacon and hams."

That decided, they stacked the lumber as they dismantled the old building, pulled out the square cut nails, and prepared a place for the smokehouse. Once the kitchen house was torn down, Kelly and Sam set to work on the smokehouse. Kelly envisioned a simple wood clapboard building. "When it is completed, Sam, the smokehouse will be 12x12 with a large hinged front door and a window cut in the back, no glass, only a shutter. The ceiling will be unsealed and open to the roof. Only the 2x4 ceiling braces visible, these will be used for hanging the meat to cure."

"That sounds simple enough to my way of thinking," Sam replied.

With the door and shutter closed, it would be black as pitch inside the smokehouse; Kelly didn't anticipate the building being used for anything else, so that was of no concern. By the first of November, the old kitchen house was gone and the smokehouse constructed.

When cold weather came to stay, the temperature a constant forty-five degrees or below, Kelly decided to butcher two of his pigs. His pa and Sam agreed to help, and so did his ma. Mary and Peninnah did the sausage grinding and stuffing. By the end of a tiring day, it was done. With the pigs, being much smaller than his pa's, the butchering went much faster.

Kelly poured sand in the bottom of one of Mary's large washing tubs, built a fire outside of hickory wood, and when it burnt down to coals, placed them into the tub. Sam helped him carry the tub inside the smokehouse. At the end of the day, the hams, shoulder portions, and the two long links of stuffed sausages were hung inside for curing. For six weeks, he added hot hickory coals to the tub to keep the smoke circulating around the hanging meat, preserving the meat for their winter lauder. Some of the meat Mary salted and layered in the salt box in the corner of the kitchen.

* * * * *

In mid-October of that year, the reality of the War in Europe was brought home to the folks of Steadman community. Leon was sitting in the schoolhouse southeast of the train depot, looking out the window, when a coffin draped in an American flag was unloaded from the train. The coffin sat on the depot platform for what seemed like an hour to a young boy before it was loaded on a farm wagon and taken away. It was the body of a young soldier, Ed Williams, who had died of pneumonia at Camp Jackson, South Carolina. Almost a month later, Leon saw another flag-draped coffin unloaded at the depot. It was the body of another young soldier, Lee Williams, who was killed in Mont Pointe, France, that had been shipped back home for burial. The two were brothers who died exactly two months apart, both buried in the Pine Grove Church cemetery.

The image of those two flag-draped coffins would remain with Leon the rest of his life. The fact they were brothers who died in service to their country was, to their neighbors, a double tragedy. Previously the War, being fought in foreign lands thousands of miles away, was only read about in newspapers; now it had actually touched their lives.

On November 11, 1918, the armistice was signed in a railway car in the Compiegne Forest north of Paris, France. World War I had come to a close and American soldiers were coming home.

Twenty-Five

TO FARMERS AND COUNTRY FOLKS JUST GETTING BY, THE passage of time is marked by seasons, not by days or months. Living off the land the way the Gantts did, their whole existence depended on the amount of sunshine, rain, heat, and cold the seasons brought. Each year began with two months of winter, freezing temperatures and blankets of frost covering the ground. Most years, at least one ice storm would paralyze activities for a few days. A cold rain with freezing temperatures left a coating of ice on the porch steps. Trees were bent over with the burden of ice, causing the limbs to splinter and break. Icicles a foot long hung from the eaves of the house, barn, and smokehouse. Whenever an ice storm hit, there was nothing to do except huddle around the fire indoors and pray for warmer temperatures.

"When the cold finally recedes," Mary noted, "and spring finally brings some sunshine, I can't help but rejoice thinking we have survived another winter of cold wind, icy rain, and heavy frost covering the ground."

At long last, March arrived. Spring couldn't be far behind; the season of new life began to show her face. Sunshine warmed the countryside, milder temperatures returned and the rains that fell brought the return of flowers and the time for planting crops. It also heralded the birth of new babies in the forest. Birds of all kind built nests to lay their colored or speckled eggs in; soon, hatchlings were learning to spread their wings and fly. It seemed the earth it-self had awakened from the slumber of a cold winter. Trees that lay dormant in the cold sprouted new leaves, Mary's flowers pushed up through the rich soil to blossom and painted the yard like a Monet with blues, pinks, and purples. Mary loved her flowers and looked forward to their arrival, though she didn't have much spare time to cultivate flowers when the crops in the fields had to come first. She had planted three apples trees at the edge of the upper field last fall and they flourished under her touch. They were little more than twigs when she planted them, but when she realized they had taken root; she babied them through the winter, putting pine straw around them and even covering the young trees with croaker sacks to protect them from the cold.

"My apple trees actually survived the winter," Mary told Kelly with a smile. "When I uncovered them, I noticed little buds begin-ning to pop out; we may just have some apples one day."

"Everything you plant, Mary, seems to be a success," Kelly not-ed. "Even those apple trees. I thought for sure you were wasting your time, but apparently not. Some people just have a special way when it comes to making things grow."

"Thank you, Kelly, that sounds like an appreciative compliment to me."

The fields had to be plowed and the seeds planted. As soon as the seeds were in the ground and sprouting, their lives revolved around their crops. There were weeds to be chopped or they would take over the fields. The terraces between had to be kept up to prevent the tender plants from being washed away in some spring cloud burst. Mid-summer, their garden came in and required constant attention as they picked and cleaned the vegetables. The excess was canned in quart jars for the winter to come and the fields of corn were ready to be picked. By the end of September, the cotton, wheat, and oats had been harvested.

"I swear, farmers have no free time if they are to be successful; that's why me and the boys drank so much on the weekends. We have to have some time to relax and enjoy each other's company. I hope you understand that, Mary. I realize you don't get time to socialize with the neighbors or visit, except church and trips with the children to Rayflin. Remember, I do appreciate all you do and I couldn't make a go of things without your help and understanding' you are my help mate. You and our children are the most important things in my life; please don't think it's the drinking."

Kelly was working at the chalk mine, but his fields still required his attention. He was a farmer first and his job at the chalk mine was only for the money. He didn't enjoy his job there; he missed being in his fields every day. When he came home in the evenings, he would walk over his fields to check the progress of the crops. Mary stayed busy from daylight to dark; she picked prepared and canned vegetables from her garden. Louise and Leon worked by her side, baby Elsie playing in the shade at the end of the garden.

* * * * *

In July of 1919, another worry presented itself. Mary suspected she was pregnant once again She had felt poorly for about a week, then the morning sickness hit and she knew. When she told Kelly about the baby, he was, of course, pleased.

"But Kelly, I'm not a young woman any more. By the time this baby arrives, I'll be thirty-six years old; this has got to be the last. It's just too hard on my poor body to keep having babies and working from daylight to dark in this house and these fields," she said, spreading her hands palms up for emphasis. "The three we have almost wear me out. Believe me, I love them dearly, but as the Good Book states, 'the spirit is strong but the body is weak'. At least, my body is."

"Well, Mary, what can I do about that?" Kelly asked with a glint in his eye. "You know how irresistible you are: babies are sometimes the result."

She didn't take too kindly to that last remark, considering she suspected he had been unfaithful with Dorothy Gunter. Pretty strong evidence had been presented to her, but she just let sleeping dogs lie. She had three children and another on the way. Women, Mary included, were forced to turn a blind eye when they had children and were dependent on their husbands for their livelihood. *Men are such predictable creatures,* she thought. *Kelly is no different than other men when it comes to loose, attractive women and their charms.*

"Kelly, I didn't mean to imply any fault on your part. I'll love this baby just like the others; I just hope this will be the last is all I meant. Whatever the good Lord intends, that's what will happen."

* * * * *

Cotton-picking time that fall, Mary and the children were helping in Jule and Corrie's fields. No matter Mary's condition, she was a hard worker and any task was given her undivided attention. Corrie was picking two rows, Mary was picking two, Leon and Louise had a row together, and Corrie's two girls, Nina Lee and Sis, had a row together. Elsie was too little to be responsible for picking; she trailed along with Mary, pulling a tuft of cotton and adding to her mother's sack every so often. When Leon and Louise were working with their mother, she didn't intend for them to dawdle. Nina Lee and Sis started playing around and getting further behind; they were hitting each other with their cotton sacks, laughing and having fun. Leon and Louise were too tempted when they saw how much fun their cousins were having and begin to swat each other with their sacks. They were getting further behind in their picking.

"Leon and Louise, catch that row up," Mary admonished them with a stern glance.

They straightened up for a little while; Nina Lee and Sis were getting further and further behind. Corrie didn't say anything to her girls; she just ignored their play and picked. Pretty soon, Leon and Louise could stand it no longer; they started fooling around again.

"Leon and Louise, I said catch that row up and quit playing," Mary said for the second time.

They picked for a while in silence and then the laugher behind them took over and the play started again. This went on for several minutes. Mary didn't say a word. She pulled up a cotton stalk and wore Leon and Louise's bottoms out with it. That ended the play and they concentrated on the job at hand.

That was the character of Mary Gantt. No matter how much work she had to do at her house, she was always willing to help the rest of the family with their crops whenever they asked. She loved her children, but they would behave themselves and mind their elders. Instilling good character and Christian values in her young children she considered her hardest and most important job.

* * * * *

After the fall harvest, school started up again at Steadman; Louise and Leon rushed out the door each morning; sometimes, as they ran up the walkway to the road, the first bell from the school could be heard as a vague clanging in the distance. It rang every school morning at 7:15 a.m. School began at eight. They ran most of the way to Aunt Corrie's, where Sis and Nina Lee joined them. Along the way, Greco Gunter, Mr. John Gunter's boy, joined the pair. Greco's younger brother, J Hugh, and Leon and Louise's sister, Elsie, were still too young for school, but it wouldn't be long before they went too. The number of students at the school was growing; they now had two teachers and there was talk of building a new school in Steadman to accommodate the increase. But that was still just talk.

Hog killing time came in mid-November and after that came Christmas. *Before we know it, the cycle of life will have begun all over and another year will have fled almost unseen before our eyes. Where does the time go?* Mary asked herself.

The year 1919 saw the passage of Prohibition. This amendment prohibited the manufacture, sale, transportation, or importation of alcoholic beverages. That only applied to legal liquor; moon shining became a profitable alternative and even though it was definitely illegal, it flourished. The Gantt brothers had been dabbling in the production of alcohol for years; soon, it would become more than a recreational pastime.

* * * * *

On the 15th of March 1920, Mary gave birth to a son. Miss Hannah attended the birth, but she was old and feeble and brought her successor, Miss Willow, to deliver the baby. Willow was Miss Hannah's daughter-in-law, having recently married Miss Hannah's widowed son, Jimmy. The birth was fairly quick, only five hours, but definitely not painless for Mary. She was exhausted by the time Ira Quinton arrived and felt a wave of relief when Miss Willow placed him in her arms. He was a beautiful baby and appeared healthy. The children were thrilled when they saw their little brother for the first time. Leon was especially happy it was a boy.

"Now I'll have somebody to play with, Momma, instead of just girls," Leon commented when the three stood beside the bed gazing into their sibling's face.

The birth had gone fine and Mary was up and about in a few days. Corrie came to visit with Nina Lee and Sis, and the children played in the front yard while Corrie and Mary laughed and talked in the bedroom. Mary seemed to be getting along fine until the morning of the 20th of March. She began to run a fever, accompanied by a slight cough.

"I'll be fine," she told Kelly when she noticed the concern on his face. "I've just developed a little spring cold, that's all."

But she wasn't fine. The fever only escalated and was followed by cough and chills. Miss Hannah and Miss Willow came back that evening to check on Mary. Miss Hannah told Kelly privately, "Get Doc Timmerman from Batesburg down here to take a look at Mary. I'm afraid it's pneumonia."

On the twenty-first, Dr. Timmerman made a house call and confirmed Kelly's worse fear; Mary had contracted pneumonia. "I'll do what I can, Kelly," the doctor said, "but it doesn't look good."

Dr. Timmerman pulled a shiny can of pink powder called antiphlogistine from his bag. "This is about the best thing we have, Kelly. I'll mix a little of the powder with warm water in a pan to make a paste and spread on her chest. That should help the congestion, and if we can just get her fever to break, she might make it. Praying wouldn't hurt either."

Doc Timmerman spent two days at Mary's bedside, but her condition only worsened. Kelly called Peggy; she and Tom arrived on the twenty-second to help with the older children and the new baby.

The children were completely at a loss. They knew their mother was seriously ill; she asked frequently, "Please bring my children in so I can reassure them and tell them how much I love them." As they were ushered into the sickroom, a weak smile would touch her lips. At two in the afternoon on March twenty-third, their world collapsed. Mary died, leaving a newborn baby, three devastated children ages four, eight, and nine, and a husband consumed with grief.

* * * * *

Leon sat in the front porch swing. As it moved slightly to and fro, the chains above his head made a squeaking noise; the shoes on his feet drug across the porch boards with each back and forth motion. In his desolate state, he had no inclination to move, only sit in silence. The only sounds on that late afternoon of despair were the hushed voices of adults, the tread of their feet across the porch as they came and went through the outside doors, and the quiet weeping of family and friends. Leon's face was streaked with tears.

He had cried and collapsed in a heap on the kitchen floor when Kelly had told the three their mother was gone. They had all clung to each other and cried for almost an hour. Kelly had tried to console them by saying she was with Jesus in a better place. A nine-year-old boy had no conception of death as the doorway to a better place. All Leon knew was his mother was never coming back and it hurt his very soul to face that fact.

Soon the news spread; neighbors came by to pay their respects and to bring food for the family. All the black folks who worked for the Gantts came too; they had a high regard for Miss Mary. Sibbie came with Uncle Caesar and Aunt Maggie and sat beside Leon in the swing. All she could offer was her presence; she had no words that could soothe his hurt. Grandpa Fink was there as were all the Gantt family. Kelly asked Sam and Rion to go to Batesburg and purchase a nice coffin for Mary. Kelly now sat in the backyard under the chinaberry tree, quietly accepting condolences from his neighbors but hardly hearing their words in his grief. Truth be known, he had been drinking to help steady his nerves. He felt he just couldn't face the next few days without some fortification from a bottle.

The women-folk bathed Mary and dressed her in her best Sunday dress of white cotton with a high lace collar and tucks on the bodice. It had been her favorite. As soon as Sam and Rion returned with the coffin, she was placed in it and laid out in the parlor beside the front window. It was now time for Kelly and the children to see her and say their goodbyes. The children entered the parlor, gingerly clinging to their father for support. Their mother was beautiful; she looked as if she was just sleeping with her hands folded at her waist. Each of her children touched her hand and whispered a goodbye through their tears as their aunts Peggy and Corrie led them from the room.

Mary's coffin was a dark brown polished wood with brass screws to secure the top. Some of the family would sit up beside it all night, as was the custom. The funeral was planned for eleven the next morning at Pine Grove Church. All the arrangements had been taken care of by Kel, knowing his son did not have the ability to handle any decisions in his state of despair.

The next morning, Leon woke up at first light and for the briefest moment forgot that his mother was no longer present. Then he heard hushed voices in the parlor and remembered. He refused breakfast; food was of no concern. He sat quietly in a corner of the dining room, folks coming and going all around him. Most patted his shoulder or leaned to whisper a few words of sympathy in his ear. When ten o'clock arrived, it was time to go to the church for the funeral. A two-horse wagon driven by Arthur Moore took Mary to the church; Dr. Canady, headmaster of the Edisto Academy at Seivern, preached her funeral, and she was laid to rest in the Pine Grove Church cemetery.

That evening, Kelly took the children down to his pa and ma's at Rayflin and they all spent the night there. The new baby, Ira Quinton, went home with Aunt Peggy and Uncle Tom Shealy. Kelly saw no alternative. He had to work to take care of the other three and his ma couldn't take in the new baby with all the others, her family, and farmhands to cook for. Peggy and Tom were the natural choice and they were more than willing to take the baby. Three years would pass before Kelly and the children would return to their house.

Twenty-Six

A HINT OF DAYLIGHT TOUCHED THE WINDOWPANE IN HER bedroom as Penninah turned back the covers and quietly slipped from her bed. She hurriedly brushed her long hair, winding it through her fingers, twirling the strands into a bun, and securing it with hair pins on top of her head.

A week had passed since Mary's death; it was time for Louise and Leon to go back to school. She headed to the kitchen to get their breakfast started. *The men-folk have to eat before going to the fields and the children must have a decent meal before walking to school.* It was planting time and work started soon after sun-up and ended at sundown. Outward grief by necessity had to be short-lived when hard work meant survival for farm folk. However, mourning for Mary would remain in their hearts forever.

Peninnah was responsible for cooking for her husband and sons, and at noon for their farmhands too. Kel had learned long ago more work got done if he didn't let his workers go home at dinnertime; it was too hard to get them back in the fields.

Peninnah started a fire in her cook stove, measured flour and lard in a bowl, and begin to mix up biscuits. She stood there with her hands in the flour, gazing out the kitchen window at the semi-darkness. Birds were just beginning to stir and twitter in the magnolia tree that brushed the eaves of the back porch; in the distance, she heard a dog barking but other than these noises, all was quiet. Her thoughts begin to dwell on her grandchildren and their grief. *Such babies, to have to bear the loss of their mother and now uprooted from the only home they have ever known. I'll do the best I can by them,* she thought. *I know Kelly had no choice but to bring them here. If only I were still a young woman, I could have taken the baby too.*

Shaking her head, she dismissed the notion from her head. No need to have regrets; Kelly had understood and hadn't expected that of her.

Peninnah heard Kel pour water into the washbasin in their room and splash his face; her sons begin to move around in their room and she heard Sam swear as he tripped over a chair.

"Kel is going to have to talk with them boys about their language," Peninnah thought aloud. "We've got tender ears in this house again and I don't want them hearing that blackguard talk from their uncles."

"Morning, Ma."

Peninnah turned from the table and there stood Rion in the doorway, his hair combed neatly, a clean red shirt visible beneath his bib overalls. "Good morning to you, Son," she said with a smile. "Your breakfast will be ready in 30 minutes; I'm just getting the biscuits in the oven now."

"No hurry for my sake, Ma, I'll go on up to the barn and start feeding the stock until it's ready."

"Are those two brothers of yours up?" Peninnah asked as Rion opened the screen door to the back porch. "Sam must be, I heard him cuss clean in here. You boys are going to have to watch that bad language around the children."

"Yes, Ma'am," Rion replied as he headed out the back door.

Kelly heard his ma stirring around in the kitchen. He and Leon shared a double bed in the oldest part of the house. Louise and Elsie were next door. Kelly sat up on the side of the bed and ran his fingers through his hair; he had to sit for a few minutes to get his bearings. His life had changed so dramatically in the last week; his mind still reeled from the onslaught of emotions he felt when his mind awakened each morning.

Mary's gone and she's not ever coming back to me, he thought, *but I can't be sitting here feeling sorry for myself. I've got to pull myself together for the children's sake. We have to get on with our lives.* He reached behind him and shook Leon gently. "Get on up, Son, you've got school today."

Fifteen minutes later, Kelly carried a sleepy Elsie to the kitchen; Louise and Leon walked behind him, already dressed for school. Kel, Sam, and Buck were sitting at the breakfast table drinking coffee when they made their entrance. Peninnah was standing beside the cook stove, stirring a pot of grits.

"The children will be going back to school today," Kelly said quietly. The words seemed to tumble out as he continued, "I have to get back to my job at the chalk mine.

Pa, would you see about the fields up at my house and the stock? I hate not to plant them, but with things the way they are, I don't hardly see how I can live down here, work at the chalk mine, and manage planting too." With a catch in his voice, he added, "Mary pretty much over saw the planting with Ab, Joe, and Arthur. She's not here to do that anymore."

"Don't worry, Son," Kel replied. "I'll ride up that way this afternoon and size up the situation. I don't see any reason why we can't plant your fields too. I don't mind handling the management for you. I know you need to keep that job at the chalk mine. Rest easy about the planting, we'll help you any way we can and I'll feed your stock while I'm there and milk that old cow. I'll just take one of your ma's crocks and bring the milk back down here."

After breakfast, Leon and Louise headed out the front door. It was right at seven fifteen a.m., forty-five minutes until school was to take in. They had a mile further to walk to school now since they were living with their grandparents at Rayflin. Leon and Louise did not know how to express their feelings to the grown-ups, but they could talk to each other, knowing they each felt the same sense of lost the other felt

"I still don't feel like our momma is gone," Leon said to Louise. "When I awoke this morning, I expected to hear her voice, almost imagined I did until I realized where I was and that it was Daddy beside me. She was always the first person I saw when I opened my eyes and now she's gone. Why would God take our mother?"

"I'm sure Momma's in heaven now," replied Louise. "Aunt Corrie told me she would always be there watching over us. Some things we can't change no matter how much we wish to. Momma wouldn't want us to be sad. She would want us to be good and remember all the lessons she taught us."

"You're right, Louise, and pretty smart for a kid. We'll make a pact between us. No more crying and feeling sorry about something we can't change. If Momma is watching, we'll make her proud and we'll help Daddy and take care of Elsie and ourselves," Leon said.

They stopped briefly in the road as they sealed the pact between them. "I cross my heart and promise," Louise replied. "We'll do what Momma would have wanted." From that day forward, Louise and Leon didn't waste time crying and feeling sorry for themselves; they got on with the business of living.

* * * * *

In the months that followed, Leon, Louise, and Elsie settled into life at Rayflin. Leon was old enough now to work in the fields with his granddaddy, and Louise helped her grandmother with the cooking and cleaning. Elsie was only five and still too little to have any chores. She spent her days trailing behind Peninnah, or playing by herself under the big magnolia tree beside the back porch.

Up every morning soon after daybreak, Leon and Louise walked the three miles to school at Steadman. Their daddy had made arrangements with the new conductor on the Swamp Rabbit, Frank Shelito, to bring the children home after school if the weather was bad. "The Swamp Rabbit stops at the depot in Steadman about two-thirty in the afternoon, the same time that school lets out," Kelly explained to Leon and Louise. "If it is raining, you children will run to the depot and board the train to Rayflin. I've already made arrangements with the conductor to pay him later for your fare."

* * * * *

Leon knew he always had a job waiting after school: working for his grandpa Kel on the farm. He learned to plow behind a mule during planting time; harvest time came and he took a croaker sack and headed to the fields to pick peas, cotton or whatever crops were ready. Also, in the fall, he helped clear new ground, took the wagon and hauled grubs to the woodpile, and after the corn had turned brown in the fields in late October, he hitched a mule to the stalk cutter and cut the corn stalks.

Their grandma was so busy cooking for the boys and farmhands on the place, cleaning, and washing clothes that the children practically raised themselves. Kelly was always working at the chalk mine and down at the store. True to their promise, Leon and Louise didn't dwell on the loss of their mother; they helped take care of Elsie and didn't let their thoughts linger on things they couldn't change.

They had been living at Rayflin almost a year when their Uncle Buck married Binnie Duffie. Buck and Binnie moved into a house on Kel's place on the road to Sugar Bottom. The four-room house had a porch across the width of the front and was built of pine lumber cut on the place. Van Fink had originally built the house for Corrie and Jule, almost fifteen years before, but they had only lived there a short time before moving nearer Steadman. The house had been painted white at the same time the boys had painted the home place back in '08.

Now only two of Kel and Peninnah children were still at home, Sam and Rion. Of course, Kelly had moved back in with the children, so the house was far from empty.

* * * * *

In February 1921, another tragedy struck Kelly and his children. Ira Quinton, the baby brother they hardly knew, died of crib death. Peggy had found him early in the morning of February twenty first in his crib, cold and still, gone on to be with the mother he never knew. To Leon, he was practically a figment of his imagination, a brother in name only. They had seen Quinton twice since the fateful day almost a year before. Aunt Peggy and Uncle Tom had brought Quinton to Rayflin twice on a Sunday to visit his brother and sisters and his father. Now he was gone too. Kelly went to Batesburg for the baby's funeral; Quinton was laid to rest in the Batesburg cemetery, but on his gravestone, Gantt was not attached to his name. It was if he was never their brother at all.

The same year, '21, Kelly finally got that Model T he had wanted so long. He bought it from his brother, Woodard, for $300.00. It was a 1918 model with cloverleaf body, gas tank in the rear, and a kerosene lamp on either side at the front; the two seats were covered in red leather. It was a beauty and Kelly and Sam and Rion were out every Saturday night in that Model T. Of course, the three of them were drinking heavily. Leon could always tell when Kelly was drunk; you would hear that Model T coming in low gear. By the end of 1921, Kelly was doing a lot of low gearing. The children all knew about Kelly's drinking. Leon especially was around his daddy and his uncles when they had been in the bottle. He hung around with them down at his Uncle Roston's store and accepted their drinking as a matter of fact.

* * * * *

Their Pa, Kel, did not excuse his boys drinking, or any one of his workers. Kel would give all his boys tucker about drinking. Sam, Rion, and Asia Gunter were working in one field plowing for Kel. They had all been drinking heavily the night before, Asia included.

Kel told Roston, "Those three were in the field plowing and puking at the same time. I said, "Go ahead and plow, I didn't tell you to get drunk." He had no sympathy when it came to their drinking. As soon as their dinner break was over at 1:00 o'clock, he said, "Alright boys, get them mules out, time to go back to work." All the boys would be smoking those one-eleven cigarettes after dinner: the pack had 111 over an Indian chief's head on the front. Hung-over or not, they stubbed out their cigarettes and went back to work. They knew Kel Gantt meant what he said; they never even considered arguing with him.

Twenty-Seven

IN THE EARLY PART OF 1922, KELLY REQUESTED THAT ROS-
ton and his family move into his house.

"I will have to consult with Farrie, but I believe she will be
agreeable."

"I really appreciate you moving your family up there," Kelly
responded. "It's not been easy on Pa to check on the cultivating,
feed the animals, and milk the cow in the evenings. I just can't bring
myself to go back yet. A house seems to fall apart when nobody lives
in it. All the furniture is still there, exactly the way Mary left it. You
only need to bring your personal belongings."

So it was decided. Roston, Farrie and their two small children,
Raymond and Mary Beulah moved from their house to Kelly's. Farrie loved the bigger house; the rooms were so large and there was
plenty of room for their children. She suspected there might be
another child on the way. *I'll just wait to give Roston the news until
I'm certain,* she thought to herself. *No need to get Roston's hopes up.*

In June '22, Farrie and the children were visiting at Rayflin.
Roston had some unexpected company at Kelly's house. It was late
afternoon when Rion, Sam, and Asia Gunter stopped by. Roston
hadn't gone to the store that day. Finding the store closed, they

decided to go to Kelly's house. Roston must be there, they decided, and didn't feel like opening the store.

The weather was tolerable and a breeze was blowing through the open hallway. It was constructed with doors on both ends that opened onto the front L-shaped porch facing the road and a side porch facing north. The latter overlooked a large field. The field to the north of the house was planted in soybeans, the plants full of dark green leaves almost appeared to grow overnight.

Roston had never felt like a farmer, but observing the fields from the north porch gave him a pleasant feeling of accomplishment. He was content to sit in the shade of the porch in a rocker Kelly had made, feel the warm breeze on his face and watch as the breeze swayed the soybeans in the field directly in front of him. The barn sat fifty feet away and to the left of the field. There was even enjoyment observing the old milk cow, mule, and chickens, which were running free and pecking the ground in the yard. This became a ritual Roston followed after he had finished his dinner and before going to Rayflin to run the store.

Houses were constructed with a large center hall to encourage any wind to circulate throughout the house when both doors were open, providing a cool breeze if the temperature permitted. He was already ensconced in a rocker on the north porch when the knock on the screen door at the opposite end of the hall announced he had visitors.

"Glad to have you stop by, boys," Roston said, swinging the screen door out to let them into the main hall. "I just didn't want to go to Rayflin and open the store after dinner," Roston said in way of explanation. "The fields are flourishing and I just felt like sitting outside and enjoying the breeze for a while."

Roston suggested they all retire to the north porch, where he had already taken up residence for the afternoon. "We'll have some refreshment in the form of a glass of moonshine." He really wanted to share the epiphany he had experienced about how fulfilling farming the land had suddenly become.

Sitting in the rockers on the north porch, Roston began to explain his mind-boggling change of heart towards the farming profession. "Now I can understand why Kelly loved to walk his fields and brag about the growing," Roston said. "It gives a man a sense of accomplishment just sitting here, seeing what can be done with the sweat of your own brow and with the help of our farmhands. Never thought I would be speaking sentimentally about laboring in the fields, but that's what I'm doing." With a little laugh, Roston stated, "Pa would sure be surprised."

"Surprised is not quite the word I would use," Sam replied. "How about shocked speechless? Pa would absolutely laugh his ass off at the mere suggestion that Roston loves farming."

"I know you boys are going to think I have completely lost my mind," Roston started to explain, "but I've decided being a farmer is not only an honorable occupation, but also very fulfilling."

Sam said, "Roston, you always hated farming, got out of working in Pa's fields any way you could; socializing has always been your main concern. You have got to be kidding us." Sam laughed. "You've always been the ladies' man, the big talker, liked to spread gossip. Now you want us to seriously believe you see the life of a farmer as a gratifying occupation."

"I agree with Sam," Rion added. "I believe you'll have to make a believer out of me. Oh, how's about we send Asia to the kitchen and have him just bring the jug. This declaration of yours…it is going to take several more drinks to convince me, I'm afraid. Do you mind getting the jug, Asia?"

"Shucks no, boys, Roston's making me thirsty too, with all his talk about loving farming. Hell, I help my Pa farm and I hate every blasted day of it, not to mention when I work with Mr. Kel. That man has no sympathy and no appreciation for good moonshine."

Shortly, Asia returned and all four got down to some serious drinking. Roston had made such an out-of-character declaration, they had to hear how he reached that conclusion when he had been so dead-set against it before. They laughed, talked, and made jokes about Roston's big change of heart, all the while drinking glass after glass of high-potency moonshine.

"It really is pleasant, sitting out here with you boys, sharing laughs and of course drinks. I don't mind being the butt of your smart remarks, especially under the circumstances. We have the rest of the evening; Farrie and the chaps will be staying in our old house at Rayflin tonight. She said, 'It needs a proper cleaning since we have been living here at Kelly's.' Doesn't make sense to me, it's just going to get dusty all over again just sitting there unoccupied, but you know how women think."

"No, Roston, you would be wrong about that," Sam remarked. "No man knows how women think, no use trying to figure them out either."

"I know I don't have a dog in this fight," Asia said. "You all know women don't hold much interest to me—neither do you fellows, by the way. But my ma is a pretty smart lady and she says women know what's best in most cases. Men need to keep their mouths shut; most men like the sound of their own voice and don't try to understand how much more common sense women have.

Whatever, I think I've just had too much of this good moonshine. I am beginning to slur my words a little."

"Hell, Asia, you slur your words when you're not drunk, it's no never mind to us. You're still our friend, just you understand, we do have interests in women," Rion replied. "Keep your special taste to yourself; we're not interested."

"That sure as hell is a fact," Sam said just before slipping into a drunken stupor.

"Guess I better take Sam inside and put him on the bed," Roston said. "After all, I guess I am the host of this little drinking party. Maybe we should have left that jug where it was. Help me get him to the bed, Rion, so he can sleep it off."

Once Rion and Roston got Sam to bed, they returned to the porch. It was just about twilight and it was even more pleasant to just sit and talk. Asia had disappeared, probably to relieve himself in the bushes at the edge of the yard Roston and Rion figured.

Asia Gunter was a character; he was openly a queer, as his attraction to males was called at the time, but Asia was a friend and the Gantts or no one in the community treated him badly because of it. He was a quiet, shy man except when he was drunk; on those occasions he would talk endlessly. He was accepted by the whole community. He was teased but not about being queer. He was teased because he took things so seriously and had an outlandish quip to make in any situation.

* * * *

"Well, I think Sammy boy is passed out in the backroom on the bed," Rion remarked, sitting in the porch rocker. Even in the dimming light of evening, Roston could tell Rion was all glassy eyed. *Can't hold his liquor I guess.*

After Asia had not returned, Roston decided he should find him. He could be passed out at the edge of the yard. Not locating Asia anywhere outside, Roston returned to the porch and Rion.

"I don't see Asia anywhere; I'm going to check inside." Sam was still the way they had left him in a back bedroom, spread-eagled on the bed, passed out and covered with a quilt. In the semi-darkness of the bedroom, Roston noticed movement under the quilt near the bottom of the bed. Throwing back the cover, he discovered Asia.

"Asia, get your ass off that bed, you'll have Sam's private parts red as a rooster's comb! You know if Sam finds out about you taking advantage of him passed out, he's liable to beat you within an inch of your life. Drunk or not, you know better. Sam can be an ornery son of a bitch. He wouldn't take kindly to your messing with him while he's drunk as a skunk, not in control of his facilities. Now get yourself off that bed and keep your mouth shut. For your sake, I hope Sam doesn't remember a thing. If I catch you taking advantage of any men that are too drunk to know what's happening, I'll personally kick your scrawny little ass. We have been friends a long time, let's keep it that way."

Sam didn't find out, and Asia remained an entertaining friend to the Gantts as long as he controlled his behavior.

Asia could surely be entertaining: maybe not the brightest of fellows when it came to book smarts. In fact, he was considered a little slow, but he had artistic talent. He could take a thin board and with a piece of charcoal and draw a recognizable likeness of anyone in ten minutes. He was almost an artistic genius. He was also a real accommodating fellow. If you ask him to help in any way, he was always there. He drank with all the boys and their teasing him didn't bother him in the least. He was a good sport because he always took what they said so seriously but never took offense at the teasing. Asia could always make them laugh, especially if there was liquor involved.

All the Gantt brothers teased Asia, but not to be mean or put him down. Asia said such funny things and his serious tone when they teased him about something was the main reason for the teasing. They never teased him about being queer; that was just part of him and had no bearing on things; it was just the way Asia was, and they had no problem with it.

Twenty-Eight

IN APRIL 1922, RION MARRIED RUTH HALL AND SHE MOVED into the house with Kel and Peninnah too. Ruth was little more than a child herself, only three years older than Leon. She was slender girl with long dark hair and dark eyes and fit in well with the rest of the family. Right away, she was expecting. The family was growing by leaps and bounds. Every Sunday afternoon, the clan would gather at Rayflin and Leon, Louise, and Elsie had an assortment of Gantt cousins to play with. Leon and Nina Lee, being the oldest grandchildren, were expected to supervise the others.

* * * * *

The seasons came and went. Up at daybreak and to bed soon after the sun set, the children accepted the big white farmhouse in Rayflin as their home. They had school to attend most of the year and chores every afternoon as soon as they came home. In September 1921, Elsie started first grade. The school year now ran from September to late May. They were out the door by 7:15 every morning to begin the trek to Steadman. Other children, cousins Nina Lee and Sis, Greco and brother J Hugh Gunter, and their cousins, Marveline and Clara Gunter, joined them along the way. By the time the group reached Steadman, there was bound to be at least one disagreement among them. Greco and J Hugh were pretty rowdy and enjoyed picking on the girls. It always took Leon to straighten the pair out. He liked to cut up and fool around, but he didn't stand for picking on girls. Of course, Sis had a temper and didn't mind getting in a tousle with the Gunter boys, and she could pretty much hold her own. Leon didn't have to intervene too often if the object of their teasing was Sis.

By the time Leon turned twelve years old in October 1922, he was doing a grown man's work every day he was not in school. His granddaddy Kel was becoming more dependent on Leon. He expected a lot from the lad of twelve. Leon walked behind a mule plowing all day during planting, and when harvest time came, he could pick as much cotton in a day as any of Kel's other farmhands. He was smart and a hard worker and no matter what task his granddaddy Kel gave him, he completed it without complaining. Leon's uncles Rion, Sam, and Buck helped with the farming but usually they had bigger fish to fry and were grateful Leon was there to pick up the slack. All the farmhands had a special admiration for the young man and his knowledge of farming.

He was respectful of them, a hard worker, and besides, he was Miss Mary's son, someone they had always felt kindly towards.

Willie Burkett, Sibbie's brother, had started helping in the fields. Uncle Caesar was not as spry as he used to be, so his son Willie worked more and more in the fields. Arthur Moore still lived in a shack on the place and worked for Mr. Kel, but the Hardy family, except for Joe and his new wife, Sadie, had quit the farm and moved to Batesburg with relatives.

Joe, Arthur, Willie, Leon, and Kel did most of the farming. Kel's sons occasionally helped, but not if they could find another job. They would rather cut timber and do sawmilling work if they could. Making and selling moonshine was much more profitable, but they had to keep that business secret from Kel. Leon was becoming an accomplished farmer. After all, he was taught by the best: his grand-daddy, Kel Gantt. As long as Leon, Arthur, and Willie were in the fields, Kel didn't concern himself with searching for stills. He was no fool and figured the boys were dabbing in the production of liquor, but the farm work was being taken care of, so he let it slide.

Twenty-Nine

SHE WAS QUIET, SHY, AND THIRTY-FIVE YEARS OLD WHEN Kelly Gantt first took notice of her. Her name was Florence and she was the eldest of eleven children born to Mr. Tom Burkett and his wife, Ella. She had never been married and was considered an old maid, but she was an attractive woman at five foot four inches tall and with dark hair and gray eyes. The Burketts had always been sharecroppers, living on somebody else's land, in somebody else's house, never having a place to call their own.

Mr. Tom had died in 1913, on Christmas Day, leaving Ella and their seven surviving children to get by the best way they could. Tom had been a good man and a hard worker. At the time of his death, he was buying the house they lived in and twenty-five acres of land from Bill Asbill over near Samaria. The debt had almost been paid, but not quite. Asbill made Ella and the children move after Tom died because they couldn't pay the balance by one bale of cotton. Asbill claimed it was the principal of the matter; the agreement had not been fulfilled and all debt had to be paid for them to remain.

Being peaceable and non-confrontational people, the Burketts just packed up and moved as Mr. Asbill had required. Afterwards, the Burketts lived wherever they could find a place and the boys, Bunyan, Will, Eugene, and James, sharecropped for local landowners or saw milled, anything they could do to bring in some money. They were not illiterate or trashy people, just poor.

Kelly always respected Mr. Tom and liked Will, Bunyan, James, and Eugene. When Kelly and his brothers Rion and Sam were out driving the countryside drinking, they would sometimes stop by to visit with the Burketts.

"How about sharing a little drink with us?" one of the Gantt brothers would ask.

And one of the Burkett brothers would agree, "Why not? Just one will be fine."

Sometimes they would share a drink. Miss Ella didn't approve of the drinking, but she liked the Gantt boys. They were always mannerly and respectful of her and her girls, Florence, Kathleen, and Rosalee. They were an entertaining bunch and always made her laugh. The Gantt brothers especially admired Miss Ella; she had an infectious laugh, loved a good joke, never once admonished them for their drinking, and even let a swear word slip every once in a while.

"I love to be around Miss Ella as much as her sons," Kelly remarked to Sam and Rion. "When she laughs, her blue eyes twinkle and she is such a good sport. She doesn't seem to mind our having a little drink at her house; she's not judgmental at all and always seems happy, even in their poor circumstance. I'm always reminded when I'm around her that material things are not what make a body happy."

Ella first noticed Kelly had an interest in Florence one Sunday afternoon when he stopped by alone to visit; none of the boys were home and Kelly stayed and sat with Florence on the porch swing talking. He made Florence laugh, which was a good thing to Ella. Florence wasn't getting any younger; here was a handsome man with a home of his own, albeit a widower with children, from a good family that seemed to enjoy just being with her daughter. By Christmastime 1922, Kelly would stop by often, sometimes with his brothers Sam, Rion or Buck, but just as often by himself. Buck and Rion were married by this time, but they still liked to ride the roads together and share a bottle.

Kelly and Florence talked about his job at the chalk mine, his farm, and most of all about his children. Florence loved children; she had helped raise her younger brothers and sisters. Her baby sister, Rosalee, was twenty-five years younger than herself and Florence sometimes felt like Rosalee was her own. She had already made up her mind: *If Kelly proposes marriage, I will accept.* She didn't like the fact he drank so much, but felt she could deal with his drinking in exchange for a home, hopefully children of her own, and a man that would love and care for her.

Kelly had made up his mind about Florence too; he had even told Roston. "I'm thinking about proposing to Miss Florence Burkett. "She's a fine lady, and I believe she would be a good wife and mother to Leon, Louise, and Elsie."

"I think that's a fine idea," Roston replied. "Do you think Miss Florence will accept, or has she heard rumors about what a big jackass you can be and how much you like your liquor? I have a feeling she is really too good for you brother, but you will be lucky if she does except your proposal. Farrie, the chaps, and myself can move back down to our old house right away. Like you said, we only brought our personal belongings. We can move easily in two days.

You might want to show Miss Florence the house before you pop the question."

"Thanks, Roston, I appreciate your doing that."

Thirty

ONE SUNDAY AFTERNOON IN LATE JANUARY 1923, KELLY stopped by the Burkett house to visit and see Florence. They didn't sit on the porch that afternoon; it was windy and cold and rain clouds had hovered overhead since noon. They sat in the front room with her mother Ella and sister Rosalee. Her brothers James, Will, and Eugene were visiting their brother Bunyan and his children. Bunyan's wife, Eula Lee, had died giving birth to their son, and they thought he could use some company.

Florence could tell there was something on Kelly's mind, but they had no privacy, so she couldn't ask what he was thinking, not in front of her mother and sister.

Finally, Kelly said, "Miss Ella, if it is ok with you, I would like to take Florence for a ride and show her where my home is and where my parents live."

"That's fine with me, Kelly, but I think Florence is the one you should ask."

"How about it, Florence, would you like to go for a ride in my Model T and I'll show you Rayflin and my house?"

"I would love to see your house, Kelly, and Rayflin. I've heard so much about it."

Kelly helped Florence into the front seat of his Model T and they headed for Rayflin. As soon as Kelly closed the door, big drops of rain began to splatter on the windshield and the wind picked up a bit. It was only four miles from Samaria to Rayflin, just three to Kelly's house. By the time they reached Kelly's, the rain was coming down in torrents. He had not intended to stop, only pass by.

Kelly just planned to point out the house to Florence and head on down to Rayflin and introduce her to his folks. He changed his mind abruptly and decided they should pull in and wait for the rain to let up. As soon as he stopped the automobile, he jumped out and ran around to help Florence. Then they both made a dash for the front porch and cover, laughing as they shook the rain from their clothes and wiped their feet on the porch mat.

"We better get inside," Kelly said as he opened the kitchen door. "Florence, wait here until I get a lamp lit."

It was only about three in the afternoon, but with the storm breaking all around them, it was dark and gloomy inside.

"Let's just sit here at the kitchen table and talk until the rain slacks up. I'll build us a fire in the fireplace. I'm sure there is dry wood still in the box on the porch."

As Kelly knelt on the hearth to start a fire to ward off the chill of that cold Sunday afternoon, Florence just sat and took in her surroundings.

In Florence's eyes, the kitchen was a dream. *It is a nice big room too, with a fine wood cook stove in the corner, a dish cabinet, a washstand for the water buckets, and a table and chairs. What a nice kitchen this would be for any woman.*

As soon as Kelly got the fire going, they pulled their chairs close to the fireplace and just sat for ten minutes, each filled with apprehension, not knowing what the other would say, listening to the rain hammer on the tin roof, watching the flames, and feeling the heat. Behind them, the room was still cold and every so often, they both stood, turning their backs towards the fire to warm their backsides. They sat there in silence, just enjoying the sound of the storm and the peace of each other's presence.

After their clothing had dried a bit, Kelly asked, "Florence, would you like to see the rest of the house before we go?"

"I would love to," she replied.

Kelly stepped back out on the porch carrying a kerosene lamp, flame flickering in the breeze even with the protection of the glass chimney. "Let me show you the newest part," he said as he led Florence to the hallway door at the end of the porch. "My brothers and I added this on in 1912; before that we only had two rooms, and with two children, that just wasn't enough space."

They stepped into the wide hall and peeped into each of the four adjoining rooms. All the furniture was still there, but most was covered with sheets against the dust that would settle into every crack and cranny over time.

"You and your brothers did a fine job, Kelly. And such spacious rooms; I can't imagine having so much room. You know how small the house we're living in is, and with all of my family, it's awful crowded."

After admiring the newer section, Kelly and Florence again crossed the porch to enter the kitchen. The rain had not abated; Kelly decided they should wait out the worst of the storm before getting back on the road.

"Let's just sit here at the kitchen table and talk until the rain lets up. I'll build up the fire in the fireplace; there is more dry wood still in the box on the porch."

They sat there in the warmed kitchen, windows steamed up inside due to the heat from the fire. Just sitting together, listening to the noise of the storm, was a comfort to both Florence and Kelly. The mutual silence put Florence at ease. Always a shy woman, she felt at peace and content with Kelly by her side. Finally, Kelly reached over and took Florence's hand in his.

"There's something I've been wanting to say to you, and I guess now is as good a time as any. You know, Florence, neither of us is kids anymore and since Mary died, I've been a lonely man. I have three children that depend on me but they need a woman to help with their raising. Ma has done her best by them, but she can't devote much time to the children with all her responsibilities on the farm."

At this point, Florence was thinking, *Please say what you want to me. Quit beating around the bush: if you want to propose to me, just do it.*

Finally, Kelly, after what seems like forever to Florence, asked, "Would you consider becoming my wife? The children need you, and I need you too. I promise to be a good husband, to love you and take care of you." Kelly had managed to get the words out.

Florence didn't even have to consider her answer; she had made her mind up weeks ago.

"Yes, Kelly, I'll marry you and I'll take care of you and your children the best I know how. I just hope they can accept me; it's hard for children when they lose their mother to take to a new woman in their daddy's life."

"They'll be fine with it, Florence, I'm sure, and you've made me very happy accepting my proposal," Kelly said as he leaned over and kissed her on the cheek. It was the first time he had kissed her, and she was thrilled. Florence, at thirty-five, hadn't had a lot of beaus and very few kisses, to her credit. A quiet smile lit up her face and a pink flush spread upward from her neck.

"Florence, I believe you're blushing," Kelly said with a grin. "How about we get married next weekend? No use putting a thing off, once you make up your mind."

They sat quietly for a few moments, holding hands in front of the flickering fire. Each was lost in thoughts about their lives together and the gravity of their decision. Florence and Kelly both were thinking about his children, Florence uncertain if she could begin to measure up to the memory of Mary, and Kelly wondering what the children would think of this turn of events. The sound of the rain suddenly diminished from a hammering to a soft 'rat-a-tat' on the tin roof above their heads.

"I guess I best be getting you on home before it gets dark; we'll visit the folks next weekend," Kelly said. He squeezed Florence's hand and stood. "I need to douse this fire; can't leave it unattended or we won't have a house to come home to."

They were both standing in front of the fireplace, and Kelly put his arms around Florence and gave her a hug. "Better stand back a bit. I'm going to stir the coals and pour on some water." He walked to the washstand and filled a dipper with water from one of the water buckets. Taking the poker, he stirred the hot coals and poured the contents over them. A thick cloud of steam rose from the hot coals, filled the fireplace, and went up the chimney. "I think it's safe now; let's go while the rain has let up."

* * * * *

The following Sunday, February 4, 1923, Kelly Gantt married Florence Burkett. Mr. A.B. Quattlebum, notary republic, performed the ceremony in the Quattlebums' parlor in Steadman.

Kelly had not confided in any of his family about their plans, only Sam. Roston was made aware of his intentions, but didn't know they had come to fruition so quickly. Kelly had asked Sam to stand up for him at the ceremony.

Sam and Kelly arrived at the Burketts soon after two that afternoon to collect Florence and Miss Ella. Florence was wearing her best Sunday dress, an ivory lace with a high neckline and a pair of her momma's shoes. She carried a lone pink Camilla, the only flower blooming in Miss Ella's yard in February. The ceremony was brief and then they returned to the Burketts to have a little celebratory drink with Florence's brothers. Of course, the little drink turned into several and before Florence and Kelly departed with Sam for Rayflin to inform the folks, Kelly was quite inebriated. Miss Ella had baked a cake for the occasion, which had yet to be cut, so she insisted they take it to the Gantts and share it with his folks.

* * * * *

Leon, Louise, and Elsie were dressed for bed when they heard their father's Model T coming in low gear.

"That's Daddy, sure as shooting," Leon said. "I wonder where he has been all afternoon." They heard steps on the front porch and then the door opened and in came a lady dressed for Sunday church carrying a cake.

"Well, Ma, I've brought you a new sister-in-law," said Kelly. He was definitely boozy and meant to say daughter-in-law. That's when the children met their new stepmother, Miss Florence. They had not a clue. While the cake was cut and served, the grown-ups talked. The children were happy to have a slice of the cake Miss Florence brought, but were not happy to have a stepmother. They didn't know what to think of this quiet, demure woman sitting beside their father. She looked pleasant enough, and when she smiled, her eyes twinkled, but she was mighty mysterious to the three children sitting across the table.

She was the one thing they had never even thought they would have to deal with: a stepmother.

Thirty-One

AFTER THE CHILDREN HAD EATEN THEIR CAKE, THEY COULD only sit and gaze at this new lady, evidently a complete revelation to them and to their grandparents. They had no idea their father Kelly had any lady friends, must less one of such high caliber.

Leon, schooled by hanging around his uncles, had no such illusions. He knew all about the birds and the bees, and knowing his father liked women, suspected these were not in the same category as Miss Florence. She seemed so quiet, kind, and not the flamboyant, foul-mouthed painted ladies that Kelly and his uncles were usually attracted to. The children, including Leon, could only sit speechless and observe as the grown-ups talked.

Leon, at the tender age of thirteen, paid close attention to his father while sitting around the kitchen table. He noticed his father, even in his drunken state, treated Miss Florence like a real lady, even having coffee with the cake she cut and served to him, the children, and Kel and Peninnah. He hadn't even suggested anything stronger to drink. To Leon, that was a sign Miss Florence was someone special.

To Leon's way of thinking, Miss Florence must be a lady and could only be an improvement for his father. Their grandparents seemed to be pleased and evidently knew something of Miss Florence's family and background. Kel and Peninnah asked Florence several questions about her family and how they were doing. She answered their questions quietly and respectfully but didn't elaborate. Miss Florence was evidently a very shy person. She asked no questions in return, just smiled mostly. After Kelly and Florence departed, presumably to spend their first night together at Kelly's old house. Peninnah shooed the children off to bed.

"You three have got to get some sleep; tomorrow is a school day," Peninnah said. "Don't dawdle. Go to sleep and don't be dwelling on Miss Florence. She was a surprise, I admit, but Kelly made a good choice. You three will get used to her, and she will be good to you, trust me. Both Kel and I agree, Kelly has gotten the best side of the bargain."

When Elsie and Louise crawled under their covers, they heard a soft tapping on their door.

Louise jumped out of bed, cracked open the door, and grabbed Leon by his nightshirt, whispering, "Get in here and be quick about it, we don't want Grandma to hear."

"You know we have to talk about this turn of events," Leon whispered as the three huddled crossed-legged in the middle of the girls' bed.

They had never in their wildest dreams thought their father would remarry, especially without giving any notice at all.

"What are we going to do?" Elsie asked. "What if Miss Florence turns out to be a wicked stepmother like in Cinderella?"

"For God's sake, Elsie," Leon replied. "You're such a baby. That's just a silly story. Even Grandma said that Miss Florence was a nice person, and I could tell by watching Daddy, even though he had been drinking, he respects her. You know what a big drunk Daddy is when he's not working; just maybe Miss Florence will change him for the better. He needs a decent woman, and to be honest, we need her too."

In a whisper, Louise asked, "Do you think she will insist that we call her Momma? I don't think I want another Momma."

"No, Louise, I don't think she will expect that of us," Leon answered. "I think she just wants us to like her. We just have to give her chance and treat her with respect. She will be kind to us, I'm sure. She will, after all, be the lady of the house. Y'all try to get some sleep and don't worry. Everything will be fine."

Leon crept silently to the door and cracked it open ever so slowly. Turning to his sisters, still sitting up in bed, he whispered "Coast is clear, good night." Closing the door he returned to his own bed next door.

Lying in his bed, Leon thought about the surprise Kelly had sprung on the whole family. *Miss Florence is a kind woman, I can just tell, he thought. Finally we're going to return to our house. I have missed home so much.* Then he drifted off to sleep.

Photographs

Original old house Kelly and his brothers built in 1912

Original old house Kelly and his brothers built in 1912

Woodard Gantt

Mary Gantt holding Leon and Louise at political meeting

Louise, Elsie and Leon

Florence and Kelly Gantt

U. Kelly Gantt   George Gantt

Kelly Gantt and cousin, George Gantt

Florence Burkett Gantt

Sam and Woodard Gantt

Virginia 'Jennie' Gantt Rish

Delphin Delmas 'Buck' Gantt

Original home at Rayflin (left to right: Roston, Cyrus, Sam,
Corrie, Kelly Gantt, background their father - Jacob Kelly 'Kel' Gantt)

Corrie Gantt Smith

Peninnah Woodward Gantt

Jacob Kelly 'Kel' Gantt

Rion Gantt

'Buck' Gantt

Roston Gantt

'Kel" and Peninnah Gantt, child is Woodard Gantt

Peggy Fink Shealy, sister of Mary, Kelly's first wife

Mary Gantt and sisters

Left to right: Woodard, Kelly, Cyrus and Sam Gantt

Uncle Cyrus's turpentine still in Alabama

Selected Sources

Book One

Buchner Sr., William J. *The Swamp Rabbit Its Time And Its People.* Self Published. 1990

Narratives

Recorded & Written Stories From Two Major Characters. Leon O. Gantt & Robert K. Gantt. All Stories Based on True Events.

About the Author

Kathy Gantt Widener was born in Lexington County, SC in the small town of Batesburg. One month after graduating from high school, she married the love of her life and spent the next seventeen years raising their three children. At age nineteen she developed an obsession for genealogy and spent endless hours in cemeteries, archives, courthouses, and interviewing older family members. After eighteen years she decided to attend college part time. In 1990 she received an Associates Degree with high honors, her major was history. Kathy and her siblings grew up in the same old house built by her granddaddy, Kelly Gantt, and his brother in 1912. Kathy and her siblings grew up listening to their Uncle Leon's stories about his youth, making moonshine and his service in WWII. Uncle Leon had a phenomenal memory and loved to share his stories. He kept Kathy and her siblings mesmerized for hours with his tales. After his death in 2002 at age 91, Kathy decided these stories deserved to be shared and began to weave them into a narrative based on true events and real characters.

The Gantt Family Tree

Jacob Kelly 'Kel' Gantt (1856 - 1930) m. Penninah Woodward (1860 - 1949)

Thomas Roston Gantt (1878 - 1951) m. Farrie Fable Jeffcoat (1894 - 1933)
- Raymond Alton Gantt (1918 - 1962)
- Mary Beulah Gantt (1920 - 2010)
- Cora Lee Gantt (1923 - 2007)
- Florrie Edith Gantt (1924 - 1999)
- Margaret Louise Gantt (1925 - 2007)
- Charles Lindbergh Gantt (1927 - 2004)
- Thelma Alma Gantt (1930 - 1997)

Jacob Cyrus Gantt (1881 - 1965) m. Beulah Louise Vann (1888 - 1981)
- Joseph Cyrus Gantt Jr. (1920 - 2005)
- John Vann Gantt (born 1924)
- Lena Moore Gantt (born 1929)

Ulysses Kelly Gantt (1883 - 1950)
1. Mary Ola Fink (1883 - 1920)
- Leon Odell Gantt (1910 - 2002)
- Louise Gantt (1911 - 1924)
- Elsie Juanita Gantt (1915 - 2006)
- Ira Quinton Gantt (1923 - 1924)
2. Florence Burkett (1887 - 1974)
- Robert Kelly Gantt (1923 - 2015)
- Nathan Byron Gantt (1927 - 1930)

Corrie Ella Gantt (1886 - 1964) m. Julian 'Jule' Smith (1884 - 1940)
- Nina Lee Gantt (born 1910)
- Evelyn 'Sis' Gantt (1913 - 2008)

Samuel Layfette Gantt (1889 – 1965) m. Mrytle Lee Bryant
- Lucille Gantt

Andrew Woodward Gantt (1892 - 1939)
1. Mamie Hall (1889 - 1931)
- Cleola Catherine Gantt (1919 - 1990)
- Marvin Chalmus Gantt (1920 - 2003)
2. Eva Padgett (1911 - 2011)
- Barbara Ann Gantt (born 1933)
- Mary Eva Gantt (born 1935)

Virginia 'Jenny' Hersey Gantt (1895 - 1985) m. Olin Rish
- Virginia Rish (1917 - 1985)
- Mildred Rish (born 1918)
- George Rish (1928 - 1993)
- Kelly Gantt Rish (1930 - 1995)
- Charles Rish (1933 - 2003)

Rion Tillman Gantt (1898 - 1966) m. Ruth Hall (1907 - 2002)
- Lois Gantt (1922 - 2006)
- Florrie Gantt (born 1925)
- Adell Gantt (born 1927)
- Amilee Victoria Gantt (born 1929)
- Vernell Gantt (born 1932)

Delphin Delmas 'Buck' Gantt (1900 - 1935) m. Binnie Duffie (1905 - 1989)
- Jacob Byron Gantt 'JB' (1921 - 2003)
- James Cromwell Gantt (1923 - 1956)
- Vivian Gaynell Gantt (1928 - 2008)

CPSIA information can be obtained
at www.ICGtesting.com
Printed in the USA
FFHW022008091218
49806378-54313FF